C*hristmas*

# On

# Pointe

# By

# Samantha

# Chase

### *To My Favorite Romance Chasers*

Another year together!

It is hard to believe that I am coming up on five years of doing this and some of you have been a part of this journey since the beginning. That still blows my mind.

Your friendship is invaluable and I am beyond thankful for each and every one of you. I look forward to the coming year and for us all and this is just my little way of saying thank you for all that you do.

So once again, this book is for you.

xoxo

*Samantha*

# One

Abby Foster ran down her snow-slicked driveway and mentally cursed her inability to keep track of the time. She'd purposely asked for the mid-morning shift at the diner because she couldn't seem to get herself there on time for the early morning one and now here she was, still running late.

Her alarm went off on time. She even got out of bed after only hitting the snooze button once. After that, it all went downhill.

Well, maybe downhill wasn't the right word. When she woke up, she put on some music and danced herself awake. Some people drank coffee; Abby danced. It was an odd habit – she was well aware – and yet it worked for her.

With October ending, she felt okay with pulling out a Christmas music CD to dance to this morning. It was inspirational and she was already thinking about her selections for the annual Silver Bell Falls Christmas Show. Her students – who were all under the age of ten – were going to love it. There would be no Nutcracker for her class. Nope. Abby believed in doing something original that would guarantee the good people of Silver Bell would want to come back year after year just to see what her tiny dancers could do.

Climbing into her car, she smiled. It was bitterly cold with snow on the ground and normally that didn't really hit until November, but Mother Nature decided to come and say hello a bit early this year. Not that she minded – the cold, the snow…it was all part of the appeal of living in the far North.

Glancing at the dashboard clock, she saw it was five minutes till nine and sighed. "Late again." Even though she knew no one would give her grief about it, she hated that she couldn't seem to be on time for anything.

Again, maybe anything was a bit strong. She managed to be on time when it was something she *wanted* to do – like teaching dance to her students. For that she even managed to be early. Of course, it could have something to do with the fact that she loved the makeshift dance studio and it afforded her way more space to move around than her own tiny basement.

So really, the diner was the job she had out of necessity – Lord knew she had enough bills to pay – but dancing was the job of her heart. She just wished she could make it a full-time job. The studio where she taught was really just a room in the community center. If she had her way, she'd build a real one with several large rooms and a stage for rehearsals and she'd teach ballet and jazz and modern dance and even hip-hop to people of all ages!

Pulling into the parking lot of the Silver Bell Falls diner, she sighed again. It was time to stop living in her dream and focus on reality. The diner – that was her reality. She needed this job and the last thing she wanted was to give her bosses any reason to cut her loose. They had been gracious enough to let her adjust her hours in hopes of her being on time, yet here it was on the third day with the new schedule and she was already late.

Running across the parking lot, she almost slipped and fell – cursing the fact that she hadn't put on her snow boots and opted for her sneakers. With a mild screech, she caught herself just before she slammed into the glass front door.

It took a moment to get her heart rate back to normal and once it was, she opened the door and stepped inside.

"That was a close one!" Bev, one of the waitresses, called out. "I thought for sure you were going to body slam the door."

Chuckling, Abby walked by as she pulled off her hat and mittens. "I'm not gonna lie. I was bracing for impact." Walking into the back room, she put her personal belongings into her locker and then pulled out her apron and tied it around her waist. She checked her reflection in the mirror and fought against sighing. Her jet-black hair was pulled back in a severe ponytail and even then it was halfway down her back. Turning back to her locker, she pulled a couple of pins out of her bag and quickly twisted her hair up into a bun.

Typical ballerina, she thought.

The little bit of makeup she wore didn't do much for her either.

"No wonder I can't get a date," she muttered as she closed her locker and made her way out to the dining area. Within minutes, she was filling salt and pepper shakers and wiping down the counters.

"Are you looking for a date?" Bev asked as she stepped closer. "Because if you are, my nephew…"

"No!" Abby quickly interrupted. This wasn't the first time Bev had attempted a little matchmaking. "I mean…no. I'm not looking for a date."

"But that's what you said when you came out here."

*Crap.* "I just noticed that I look a little…blah…when I looked in the mirror." She stopped and gave a soft laugh. "Especially when I have my hair pulled back and no makeup on." She shrugged. "Just an observation."

"Well, if you change your mind…"

"How was the breakfast crowd this morning? Any good gossip?" *Please let there be gossip*, she silently begged.

"Just the usual. Kay Farrell and JoDeen Martin were arguing over who is running the quilting bee."

"Again? Aren't they co-chairs?"

"Yup. And they're both still trying to figure out who is the head co-chair."

Abby smiled and moved on to filling the napkin holders. "Any word on Hank and Lisa's new grandbaby? Is she here yet?"

"Nope. They're going to induce Aimee on Saturday so I'm sure we'll be seeing all kinds of pictures on Monday."

"Damn. And I'll miss it," she muttered.

"Are you missing your morning shift already? I thought you wanted to come in later."

"I did. I mean…I do. It's just…it's quiet in here now and the lunch crowd is always in such a rush that I don't really get to hear anything good. Breakfast is when everyone shares all the juicy stuff and all the interesting people are here."

Bev leveled her with a stare. "Interesting people? Seriously?"

"What? What's wrong with that?"

"Or do you mean *interesting* people?" she asked with a little more emphasis.

"I'm sure you're going somewhere with this, but for the life of me I don't know where."

"Oh please, Abby," Bev said with a chuckle. "You and I both know you used to enjoy watching our resident recluse and trying to chat him up when he would come in for breakfast."

"Not much of a recluse if he came in for breakfast every day," she muttered and then smiled brightly at Bev. "And I don't know who you're even talking about."

*Liar. Liar. Liar.*

She spun and wiped down the countertop, then moved on to brew a fresh pot of coffee.

"Fine, be that way," Bev said evasively, her blonde bob swinging as she turned and walked away. "Did I mention that my granddaughter Lindsay is thinking of taking your beginner ballet class?"

That piqued her interest. "Really? That would be great! We're rehearsing for our Christmas performances so now would be the perfect time!" Abby spun again before she bent down to wipe up some sugar that had spilled on the floor. Once she was on her feet and moved to toss the rag aside, she caught Bev grinning. "What? Why are you smiling?"

"It's like you do ballet without even thinking about it! I was just standing here watching you bend and glide and…move like a dancer. So graceful, so elegant…even when it's just cleaning up this place."

She blushed. It really wasn't a conscious effort; it was just the way her body moved.

Bev waved her off. "Anyway, I think my daughter wants to wait until after Christmas. There's too much going on right now with the holidays. Honestly, I don't know how she keeps track of everything between the shopping and school projects and parties…things weren't nearly this hectic when my kids were little."

Deflating a little, Abby sighed. "Well, she does a wonderful job and if she reconsiders, I always have room in the class."

"You're a sweetheart, Abby."

"Thanks."

A few customers came in and sat down and Abby went about getting them coffee and menus. After taking their orders and handing them to Dan, the diner's cook, Abby turned around and noticed Sherriff Josiah Stone walking in.

"Morning, Sheriff," she said with a smile.

"Hey, Abby. How are you?"

She immediately poured him a cup of coffee and placed it in front of him as he took a seat at the counter. "Doing well. How about yourself?"

He nodded and added a couple of packets of sugar to his coffee. "Can't complain."

"How's the house coming along? I saw a lot of trucks coming and going from your property over the last week. I bet Melanie's happy to see it starting to come together."

Smiling, he took a sip of his coffee before answering. "She is. Although, if we don't stop making changes to the plans, we're never going to get the place done. Every time we sign off on the design, we both think of something else we'd like to have." He shook his head and laughed softly. "We probably could have had the whole thing done by now if we'd just stuck with the original plans."

"I imagine that's hard to do. After all, it can't be easy to think of everything you want or need and remember to include it."

"That is the truth," he agreed.

"Hey, Josiah," Bev said as she walked over. "A little late for you to be coming in, isn't it?"

"Had to handle some official duty this morning that just about took me down," he said, his tone somber.

Both Abby and Bev stood stock-still. "What happened?" Bev asked. "No one mentioned anything during the breakfast rush."

He shook his head. "Had to deliver some bad news to a friend," he sighed, taking another long sip of his coffee. "Sometimes I hate my job. It never gets easier."

Reaching out, Bev put her hand over one of his. "I'm so sorry. Can you…I mean…are you allowed to tell us who it is and if there's anything we can do?"

At first, he shook his head and stared down at the mug in his hand. But when he looked up at them, Abby saw the anguish in his face. Whatever had happened, it was tearing the poor guy up.

"Do you remember Karen Hayes?" he asked, looking primarily at Bev.

"She went to school with my Susan," she replied. "A bit of a hell-raiser. Moved to Pennsylvania years ago, right?"

Josiah nodded. "Ten years," he said. "She moved away. Got married. Her husband was killed in Iraq about five years ago." He paused, muttered a curse. "They had a baby girl that he never got to meet."

"I remember that," Bev said quietly. "Dean went and stayed with her for a while. When he came back he was even more…what's the word…disconnected?"

"Karen was a mess, as you would expect, and it took a long time for her to start coming to grips with things so that she could focus on her little girl again," Josiah went on. "And then…a couple of years ago she started getting wild again."

"Karen was always the wild child," Bev said, shaking her head sadly. "Always in trouble in one way or another and Dean was always trying to clean up her messes. So sad. Their parents never knew what to do with her." She turned and looked at Abby. "They retired down in Florida after Karen moved away. I think they were both so tired and mentally exhausted that they found a place to start over."

"Trust me," Josiah said, "they deserved a break. They wanted to live some place where nobody knew them or their daughter so they could have a little peace."

"But what about Dean?" Abby asked. "I mean…he's their son. Didn't he factor into any of this?" This was all brand-new information to her. Dean had been several years ahead of her in school so their paths never crossed back then. But for all the time she had known Dean as an adult – well, the year or so that she had known him – this subject had never come up.

"Part of the reason he's a bit of a hermit, I'm afraid," Josiah said quietly. "I think he went in the complete opposite direction of his sister and took it to the extreme so no one could even think he'd be like her."

"So he's cut himself off from people because…what…" Abby said, slightly annoyed, "because his sister was a hell-raiser? He could have moved away too."

Even the thought of Dean Hayes not living in Silver Bell Falls was enough to make Abby's stomach clench. She didn't really know him very well, but she'd always hoped to change that.

"True," Bev interjected. "But…he loves it here. He loves the town, the weather…all of it. I just wish he could enjoy it more."

"He could," Abby murmured. "He's a grown man and after all these years you'd think the people around here would have learned he's nothing like his sister."

"Oh, people know it," Josiah said. "But…old habits die hard and I think he just got used to being alone. Even his job keeps him on his own most of the time."

"What's he do again?" Bev asked.

"Environmental engineer," Josiah replied. "You know, he goes out and…"

"Abby! Order's up!" Dan called out and she mentally cursed, not wanting to miss the rest of this conversation.

"Excuse me," she murmured and went to pick up her plates for her customers. Once she brought them their plates, refilled their coffees and made sure they had everything they needed, she walked back over to where Bev and Josiah were still talking.

"That is so sad," Bev said, her voice thick with emotion. "I just can't believe it."

"What?" Abby asked. "Believe what? What's happened?"

With a weary sigh, Josiah scrubbed his hand over his face before looking at her. "Karen died. Drunk driver."

Abby's heart actually ached. She didn't know the woman, but she knew Dean. "What about her daughter?"

"Dean's on his way there now," he replied and then rolled his shoulders as if trying to break the tension. "She was with a babysitter last night so Dean's going to go and take care of things. I'm sure he'll be gone for a couple of weeks."

"Wow," Bev said and gave Josiah a friendly pat on the arm. "That's a rough way to start your day."

"Can I get you more coffee? Something to eat?" Abby asked.

He shook his head. "No. This was just what I needed. A little break before heading to the station." He rose and gave them both a sad smile. "I'm going to be checking on Dean's property while he's gone. Maybe when he's on his way back we can arrange to have some food waiting for him."

"I'll organize it," Bev said solemnly. "Don't worry about it."

"You're a good woman, Bev. Thanks."

Just as he was turning to leave, Abby called out his name. "Is there anything else we can do, Josiah?"

Another small smile. "Until he gets back, all we can do is pray for the family and for Karen's little girl." He put his sunglasses on and waved before turning and walking out of the diner.

"Such sad news," Abby said. "Poor Dean. His poor niece! To lose both of her parents like that." She shook her head.

"As far as I know, other than Dean and his parents, there isn't any other family. I can't imagine how that little girl is going to handle living in a retirement community in Florida," Bev said as she picked up Josiah's mug and put it in the bus bin.

"You don't think she's going to come and live with Dean?"

For a minute, Bev's eyes went wide and then she laughed quietly. "Abby, does Dean Hayes strike you as daddy material?"

The flash of Dean holding a baby flickered through her mind and it was so clear that it startled her. "I, um…I guess…I don't…"

Reaching out, Bev patted her on the arm. "You're probably not the best person to ask."

Frowning, Abby turned as Bev walked toward the kitchen. "What does that mean?"

Bev turned at the swinging door to the kitchen. "You have a very expressive face and it's been hard not to notice that look of longing there whenever Dean was here for breakfast. You've been crushing on him pretty hard for a while. I think it would be very easy for you to picture Dean in the father role, but I just don't think it's going to happen."

"You can't know that," she responded with just a hint of defiance.

"You're right," Bev replied levelly. "But…history isn't pulling strong in his favor."

Once the kitchen door swung shut behind her, Abby sighed. Maybe Dean Hayes hadn't been daddy material up until now, but she couldn't imagine him simply walking away from his niece. True, she didn't really *know* him – had barely spoken more than a handful of words to him and most of them were about his food order – but she had a…feeling about him.

*A sexy feeling.*

Not the time! She admonished herself.

"Abby, can we get the check?" her diners called out. She smiled, nodded and pulled out her receipt pad to total everything up. As she walked over, she was a little surprised to find them talking about the Hayes family too.

"All I'm saying is Alan and Amber Hayes have been through so much. There's no way they can possibly take on a five year old…"

"They don't really have a choice. Who else is going to take in that poor little girl?"

"Maybe Karen assigned a guardian for her? You know, a friend or something."

"The girl should be with family – and that's Alan and Amber. It's not like Dean's going to do it."

"That's true…"

With a little more force than she intended, Abby ripped the receipt off her pad and slammed it down on the table. With a huff, she asked if she could take their plates and once she had, she stalked off.

Maybe no one else in Silver Bell believed that Dean Hayes was a stand up kind of guy, but Abby did.

She just hoped he'd prove her right.

****

Dean was exhausted. There was no other word for it. Mentally and physically, he was worn out. The week had been hellacious. The funeral. His parents. The paperwork.

And Maya.

He had no idea what he was doing where she was concerned and yet…he had to hand it to the kid, she was fairly self-sufficient.

For a five year old.

From what he could tell, his sister had not been the greatest parent and Maya learned to do a lot for herself. And he might not know anything about kids, but he had a feeling that this wasn't a particularly good thing.

He was sitting at his sister's dining room table in the tiny apartment she'd been living in for the last few years when he heard his parents come into the room.

With their luggage.

"What's…what's going on?" he asked cautiously.

"We're heading back to Florida, Dean," his father said.

"Now? You're leaving now? Is Maya even packed?"

His parents looked at each other and then at him. "Um…Dean," his mother began, her voice small and uncertain. "We're not taking Maya with us. We can't."

"So where is she supposed to go?" he demanded, but he had a sinking suspicion he already knew.

They sat down on either side of him and he knew that look…the one where they had the capability of guilting him into understanding them. He knew this was a possibility – a really slim one – and yet now that it was actually happening, he wanted to scream that enough was enough. He'd been the good child, the good son. He'd worked hard, got good grades and had a respectable job.

Then why – *why?!* – was he always having to clean up after everyone? Why did everyone else get to do what they wanted and he was the one left holding the bag?

"Dean, Maya's just a little girl. She has a lot of energy and needs," his mother went on. "We just can't give that to her. You're young and Silver Bell Falls is a wonderful place for her to grow up."

He couldn't believe what he was hearing. "I don't know shit about raising a little girl," he hissed quietly – unwilling to let Maya hear this conversation. "Why can't she stay with you for a little while? Just…just through the holidays? That will give me time to get things situated back home and who knows? Maybe you'll find that you want her to stay with you."

"It's not going to happen, Dean," his father said, his voice quiet but firm. "Maya needs to be in school and we live in a retirement community. There are no children there for her and the nearest school is far enough away that she wouldn't even get a bus. Taking her to live with you is the most practical way to go."

Jumping up he looked down at his parents. "To hell with being practical!" His voice rose and for a moment he didn't care. "There has to be another option! I came here and I handled all of the funeral arrangements. I'm handling all of the damn legalities and getting Karen's shit in order. You can't lay all of that and a kid on me!"

"Grandma?" a small voice called from the kitchen. Dean wanted to kick himself. He just said that he didn't want Maya to hear this conversation and now look what he'd done.

Rising from her seat, Amber Hayes stood and looked at her son with disapproval before heading into the kitchen.

Dean sat back down and raked a hand through his dark brown hair. He wanted to tug it out in frustration. He wanted to scream and yell and stamp his foot and demand that someone listen to him – that someone let him have his damn life! Hadn't he sacrificed enough? As it was, he barely had a life and now…now he was supposed to be responsible for a five year old?

"Dean, I know we're asking a lot of you. And believe me, I wish there were another solution. But…she's your niece."

"She's your granddaughter," he quickly interrupted.

Alan sighed. "I want you to think about this reasonably and think about what is best for Maya."

"Two loving grandparents would be better for her than one reclusive uncle," Dean reasoned. "Hasn't Maya been through enough? I'm *not* what she needs right now, Dad."

His father studied him for a long moment before he finally spoke. "I think you both need each other."

"What?"

"Dean, you are a fine young man – no father could be prouder. But you've gone to such lengths to be the opposite of your sister that I don't think you know who you really are. You've been hiding for so damn long and it's time for that to stop. Having Maya with you will ensure that."

"Dad…"

"I know it all looks bleak right now, but once you get this apartment packed up and you head back to Silver Bell? You'll see. It's going to be a good thing."

He wasn't going to win this argument. Dean realized that now. "How…how am I supposed to know what to do? I mean, I know it looks like Maya's a pretty independent kid, but…she's going to be dealing with so much. Too much. She's lost both her parents and then I'm going to make her move and start a new school. How much can a kid that young take?"

"Honestly? I don't know. Kids are fairly resilient in so many ways, but this? I think you're going to have to go to her school, talk to her teacher and maybe get the name of a counselor in Silver Bell."

"A counselor? For what?"

"Maya may need to talk to someone – someone she can express her grief to who will understand. And maybe someone who can help the both of you bond and learn how to move forward."

"You make it sound very neat and tidy, Dad. I think there's more to it than that."

"If you're looking for a cut-and-dried answer, I don't have one. This is new territory for all of us." Alan stood. "But I do think that the key here is trying to keep things as normal as possible. Don't let her stay at home for too long. Get her back to school. Get her involved in the community. She's going to need the distractions." He paused. "And so will you."

"Dad, I really wish you'd reconsider…"

"Maya has decided that she would like to say something to all of us," Amber said as she led her granddaughter back into the room.

Dean's heart beat madly in his chest. How could he have screwed this up so fast? This tiny girl with the wide blue eyes and blonde ringlet curls looked like she had her shit together more than the three adults in the room did. She hopped up to stand on one of the dining room chairs and looked at her grandparents and then at Dean with a grim expression.

"I know Grandma and Grandpa are going back to Florida. Grandma says I can come and visit and we'll go to Disney World," Maya began. Then she looked at Dean and her gaze narrowed. "I'm s'pose to live with you now."

He swallowed hard and nodded. "Uh…that's right. You're going to come and live with me in Silver Bell Falls."

She studied him silently for another minute. "Can I have a pink bedroom?"

Her question took him by surprise. His eyes went a little wide and he looked over at his parents for approval. When they nodded, he said, "Uh…sure. We'll paint it when we get back."

"Are there kids in Bell Falls?" she asked.

"Bell Falls?"

"Where you live," she said, her tone already conveying that she thought he was a moron.

Rather than correct her right now, he nodded. "Yes. Yes, there's a lot of kids there."

"Do you like pizza?"

Seriously? Was the kid interviewing him? "I do," he replied and then decided to turn the tables. "Do you like burgers?'

"Can I have french fries with them?"

He couldn't help but chuckle at her response. "Of course."

She nodded. "I like ice cream."

"Me too. Butter pecan is my favorite."

"I like strawberry," she said, a little disappointed. "Will I have to learn to like butter pecan?"

Dean shook his head. "Nope. You don't have to learn to like it. If you like strawberry ice cream, then we'll buy strawberry ice cream."

Maya crossed her skinny arms and seemed to be thinking of her next question. "Can we go to the library?"

"Now?" he asked, a little confused.

"No, when we get to your house. Do you have a library there?"

"Uh...yes. There's a library there." He had a feeling they had some sort of kids groups and activities there. Maybe he could look into that.

"Can I bring my bike with me?"

"We're going to bring all of your things with you," he told her softly. "Whatever you want to take with you, we will."

She bit her bottom lip and then looked down at her toes. "Will...will I have to sleep at the babysitter's house all the time? Or stay in my room when you're not home?"

Beside him, his mother gasped quietly.

And in that moment, Dean's heart broke. He had his suspicions about what life was like here for his niece, but to hear her start to confirm some of his worst fears just about killed him. Moving in close to Maya, he tucked a finger under her chin so she had to look at him.

"You're never going to be left alone again, Maya. I promise. I...I don't know how we're going to make all of this work yet. This is all new to me too. But I can tell you right now that I won't make you stay anywhere that you don't want to stay. And the only time you're going to sleep out is if a friend asks you to. How does that sound?"

Her blue eyes went wide. "I'm allowed to sleep at a friend's house?" she asked with awe.

Unable to speak over the lump in his throat, Dean nodded.

Maya looked at her grandparents before giving Dean her attention again. "Uncle Dean?"

"Yes, Sweetheart?"

"Um…do you think…um…can I…"

"What would you like, Maya?" he asked gently.

She bit her lip again and for the first time since he'd arrived, she seemed uncertain of herself. "My mom always said that I had to stay home. That I had to be a good girl and be quiet and not ask for so much stuff."

Dean knew it was wrong to be angry with his sister, and yet….

"Some of my friends from school, they…they get to go to classes after school," she said quietly. "Do you think I can go to classes after school?"

He wasn't sure he understood what she was asking. "What kind of classes?"

"My friend Dawn and my friend Jackie take ballet and…and…they get to wear pink tights and tutus and whenever I asked Mommy, she said I asked for too much stuff so I couldn't do it. But Dawn would show me some of her dances and…" she jumped down from the chair and moved into some sort of pose and then another until she was practically leaping all over the dining room.

"I know I'm not very good at it," she said and then took another big leap before spinning around. "But if I go to classes, I'll get better. So can I? Can I please?"

"You want to take ballet classes?" he asked, part of him loving the look of happiness he saw on her face.

She nodded vigorously and then did a few more uncoordinated leaps around the room. "I do! I do! I really do!"

For the life of him, he had no idea how or where he was going to find ballet classes for Maya but he did know this – he wasn't going to rest until he found her one.

"Then I guess you're going to take ballet classes," he said with a big smile.

"Yeah!" she cried as she ran over and wrapped her arms around his legs and squeezed. When she looked at him, she reminded him of a cherubic angel. "Can we leave for Bell Falls right now?"

# Two

It wasn't as if she was stalking.

Not really.

But Abby found herself being more than mildly curious about when Dean was coming back to town and how he was doing. She casually asked Josiah about him whenever he came in to the diner.

Which was every day.

And maybe she asked Bev for an update when they worked together.

Which was almost every day.

And maybe – just maybe – she even drove by Dean's house to see if he was back yet. It wasn't stalking. It was…neighborly concern.

And if anyone wanted to argue her "neighborly" reference when she lived right in town and Dean's house was right on the edges of Silver Bell Falls then…so be it. He was a hometown guy and she was a hometown girl and she could argue that she was simply concerned for one of her own.

Dean had been gone for almost two weeks and as she made her way around the diner – wiping down tables and refilling the condiments – she began to wonder if he was even going to come back. Maybe there was a lot to do to settle his sister's affairs. There was probably a lot of paperwork and with a child to consider, he probably had even more paperwork to deal with.

Just thinking of the little girl made Abby's chest ache a little bit. The poor little thing – to be without the only parent she'd ever known? It must be terrifying for her. No one had mentioned the daughter or what was going to happen to her, which only made Abby even more curious.

"Table six needs their check," Bev said as she walked back toward the kitchen.

"Thanks."

It was almost three o'clock and that meant it was almost time for Abby to clock out. She did a final sweep of the diner and was amazed to see that it was almost empty. Her couple at table six were standing and once their check was paid, the place would be clear. With a smile, she told them she'd meet them at the register.

"How are things going for the Christmas show, Abby?" Millie Taylor asked. "You did such a beautiful job last year that we just can't wait to see what you've got in store for us!"

Blushing, Abby smiled. "Things are coming along. I'm working with some of the moms on costume designs and I think we may go for a fun group number with all the ages for at least one dance."

"Oh, that's going to be wonderful! Especially for the families that have more than one child dancing! What a treat!" Millie gushed. "I wish my little Caroline had an interest in ballet. I would love to see her up on the stage."

"You know, if there were something Caroline was interested in, tell her to come and talk to me. I'm always open to doing more classes."

"You're too good, Abby," Millie said with a smile and then looked over at her husband Paul. "We don't want you to over-commit. And the community center can only hold so many classes."

"Believe me, I would love to have a real dance studio and have other teachers working with me where we could have every kind of dance class imaginable – including ones for couples!"

"Couples?" Millie asked excitedly. "You mean like ballroom dancing? We always wanted to try that, didn't we, Paul?"

He nodded but didn't look overly enthused. "We watch *Dancing with the Stars* all the time and Millie swears we can look like that too with a little practice."

The gears were already turning in Abby's head. "We could even do swing dancing and country western dancing or even dancing for weight loss like Zumba! Oh, if we had the space, the sky would be the limit!"

"Abby Foster you have gotten me all excited about this! What do we have to do to make it happen?"

For a minute, Abby could only stare. Was Millie serious? "Well…um…we'd need a building. Some place that would be big enough to house several dance studios – rooms – and maybe even a stage for practice recitals. We'd need to find teachers but I don't think that would be a problem at all. I know plenty of dancers. And…"

"So why haven't we done this?" Millie asked.

*Ugh.* Where did she even begin? "It's not a simple thing, unfortunately. I know that I can't afford to build something like this and I don't think there are any existing spaces that can be transformed. Even if there were, renovations are expensive too."

"You could take on investors, couldn't you?" Paul asked, suddenly very interested in the conversation.

"I suppose. I never really thought about it. I just thought it was something only I was interested in," Abby said.

"Listen, you just leave it to me," Millie began. "I know that the whole town of Silver Bell Falls benefits from the classes you teach and the performances you do at the holidays and during the festivals. And I think if we put it out there to the masses, we can come up with something that would work."

Her heart began to beat like crazy. "I…I don't even know what to say to that, Millie. I mean…I…I…"

Millie reached across the counter and patted her hand. "Give me a week and then we'll sit down and talk," she said. "But I'm already formulating a plan!"

With a smile and a wave, Abby watched as they walked out the door. For a moment she stood there in stunned silence.  Was it possible?  Was it really something that could happen for her?  Her own dance studio?  A place where she could have more room and be able to offer even more classes?  And maybe, just maybe, she wouldn't have to work as a waitress anymore because the dance studio would be her full-time job!

With every thought that came into her head, her excitement grew.  Looking at the clock, she saw it was three – time for her shift to end.  Ripping off her apron, Abby stepped around the counter and did a happy little spin and then a grand jeté across the diner.  When she landed on her feet, she heard the bell above the diner door jingle.  Smoothing her hair and her shirt, she turned and almost gasped.

Dean was back.

And beside him was a little blonde-haired angel.

"Did you see that, Uncle Dean?  That's what I want to do!"

\*\*\*\*

For a moment, Dean didn't move.  Didn't even blink.

That move…that leap…that…*wow*.

Beside him, Maya tugged at his coat.  "Did you see her?  Did you see her?  She's a real-life ballerina!  I know it!"  Then she ran over to Abby.

Abby Foster.  Hell, he'd always admired the way she moved around the diner, but he'd never seen her do anything quite like that. It was…*damn*. It was impressive.

"Maya," he called out lamely but still couldn't bring himself to move. Instead, he stood in fascination as he watched Abby crouch down to talk to his niece.

"Are you a real ballerina?" Maya asked with awe – as one would ask Santa Claus if he was real.

Abby smiled as she looked at her. "Yes, I am. And who are you?"

"I'm Maya and I just moved here to Bell Falls…oops…I mean Silver Falls. No," she sighed dramatically and looked over at her uncle. "What town is this?"

He smiled and took a tentative step toward them. "Silver Bell Falls," he said softly.

"Right," Maya said, nodding. She faced Abby again. "I just moved…here."

"Really?" Abby said with pleasure. "Well I just know you're going to love it here! There are a ton of kids around and I know you're going to make a bunch of friends!" She stood up and smiled at Dean shyly. "Hi, Dean. Would you like a booth or the counter?"

"Um…a booth," he said, but couldn't seem to let himself look directly at her. It wasn't as if Abby were a stranger or that he'd never noticed her before – he had. Unfortunately, their interactions had been limited to him ordering his breakfast and talking about the local news. She'd always been nice to him and even those small conversations seemed to brighten his day. Of course it would make sense that she'd be sweet and friendly to Maya. That was who Abby was. Everyone in Silver Bell Falls knew Abby and how she always seemed to be there for everyone.

She was a good person.

A sweet person.

And yet he was still reeling – and a little turned on - from her little leap across the diner.

Once they were seated, Dean realized that Maya was still talking. "…and I want to get tights and a tutu and then I'm gonna learn how to jump up like you just did!"

Abby smiled and didn't seem put off by Maya's overly-enthusiastic chatter. "Well I'll tell you what, I'm just getting ready to leave here and go over to the community center where I teach ballet classes. Maybe after you eat, you and your uncle can come over and observe a class." She paused and looked at Dean. "That is…if you have time. Sorry. I should have thought of that first."

He was just about to tell her that it was all right – that bringing Maya over to the community center would really help him out a lot – but his niece beat him to it.

"We don't have *anything* else to do, right Uncle Dean? You said that we were going to look into ballet classes right away so we need to hurry up and eat so we can go and watch the class and then I can get signed up and then we can go and buy my tights and tutu and stuff!"

Without missing a beat, Abby turned and grabbed a couple of menus for them and smiled again at Maya. Picking up the menu, the little girl pretended to read it and then announced, "I'd like a cheeseburger, french fries and a strawberry milkshake!"

"Uh…Maya…maybe you should…" Dean began.

"That is a lot of food, but you know what?"

Maya's eyes went wide as she moved in closer to Abby as if getting ready to hear a secret. "What?"

"Strawberry milkshakes are my favorite." Then she ran a hand over Maya's curly little head. "Enjoy your meals and I'll see you soon."

Just as Abby turned to walk away, Maya called out to her. "Can you do that jump again? Please?"

Dean saw the uncertainty on Abby's face. "Maya, the diner probably isn't the best place for Abby to be doing that. And besides, she needs to get going so she won't be late for her class."

The little girl considered him for a moment and he knew in an instant that she didn't care for his observation. She looked back at Abby with her big blue eyes and pled. "Please? Just one more?"

Abby chuckled softly as she moved away. "Okay. But just one more and then I have to go."

She walked toward the front door and seemed to gauge her space. Dean had to admit, he really wanted to see her do it again too. If she could move like that in the tight confines of the diner, he couldn't even imagine what she'd be able to do with an empty room.

Her expression turned serious and he watched her sort of sway this way and that before taking a steadying breath. And then he watched in pure awe as she gracefully spun around a few times and then did a massive leap in the air – as if doing a split in midair!

Holy hell!

She landed elegantly on her feet, struck a dramatic pose and as Maya began to clap enthusiastically, she took a bow. She wasn't even a little bit breathless, but Dean sure as hell was!

Abby walked up to them, smiled and said, "I'll see you both soon!"

Both Dean and Maya watched as Abby disappeared through a back door. Just as he started scanning the menu, she came back out in her coat and had a cute knit hat on her head and a cheery red scarf around her neck. She waved at them one more time and then made her way out the front door.

*Damn.*

It wasn't until Bev cleared her throat that Dean realized he was still staring at the door. He looked up at her and felt heat burning his cheeks. He also noticed the knowing smirk on her face.

*Great.*

"So…any specials today?" he asked and immediately cursed the slight crack in his voice.

For the next few minutes they talked specials and Maya chatted with Bev – her voice happy and animated. For the first time in two weeks, Dean felt himself start to relax. They were going to be okay.

They hadn't even made it back to his house yet. They'd been driving through town when Maya said she was hungry. They ate breakfast late and while they were on the road, neither had been particularly hungry for lunch. As soon as Dean spotted the diner, though, his stomach protested and demanded to be fed. Knowing there wasn't going to be any food at his house for a home-cooked meal, stopping at the diner seemed like a good choice. His day was far from over, but hopefully they'd eat some lunch, make a quick stop at the community center and be home before dark.

And then it would easily be midnight before he had everything unloaded and a room set up for Maya to use.

*Dammit.*

Maybe today wasn't the best day for them to go to the community center to check out the ballet classes.

"And Abby said that she's going to make me a list of what I'm gonna need for the classes!" Maya was telling Bev. "I already know about the tights and the tutu but there are special shoes too and stuff." She took a breath before going on. "Do you think I should get a pink tutu or a purple one? Or maybe yellow! Do they make yellow ones?"

Bev chuckled and looked over at Dean with a grin. "You'll get used to it."

"Are you sure?" he asked wearily. "I'm sitting here thinking of all the things we still have to do." Stopping, he looked at Maya. "I think we should wait until tomorrow to go see Abby. We still have to get home and unpack the trailer."

Those big blue eyes instantly filled with tears and her bottom lip quivered.

Then she lowered her head and seemed to pull herself together. "Oh. Okay."

This had to be the worst feeling in the world, he thought. He looked up at Bev helplessly – silently begging her for advice.

"Like I said," she began softly, "you'll get used to it." Then she walked away to get their drinks and put in their order.

"Maya…sweetheart…I'm sorry. It's just that it's getting late and we still have so much to do. It's been a long day and a long drive and…I want us to get settled in a bit tonight. Tomorrow we'll go to the store and get things for your room and I promise we'll go to the community center and talk to Abby, okay?"

She nodded and quietly thanked Bev who put their drinks down on the table.

His gut clenched and his mind raced with how he could get everything done that needed to be done. Maybe if they only spent fifteen minutes in Abby's class it could work. Or if they ate really fast. Or maybe...

"Hey, Dean."

Dean looked up and saw Josiah walking toward him, smiling. Relief washed over him. A friend. Someone who could possibly help him with all the things he still had to do. "Hey," he said and moved further into the booth. "Good to see you."

"I've been watching for you," Josiah said as he sat down. He looked at Maya and smiled. "And you must be Maya."

She nodded solemnly and took a sip of her milkshake.

Josiah glanced at Dean briefly and then back at Maya. "So your uncle told me all about you. I'm the sheriff of Silver Bell Falls and I'm here to officially welcome you."

Maya raised her head. "Really?"

He nodded and then showed her his official badge. "I like to welcome all of the new residents of Silver Bell Falls personally. I think you're really going to like it here."

"It's cold," she said with a bit of a pout.

Josiah nodded. "It sure is. But you know what's good about that?"

"What?" Now she looked mildly interested.

"We get lots of snow and then we all ride our sleds and build snowmen and have a whole lot of fun. Do you like building snowmen?"

She shrugged.

It only took a second for Josiah to catch on. "How about this? The first time it snows, I'm going to come over and help you build one. What do you think?"

"Okay." There was little to no enthusiasm in her response.

Dean was just about to beg for mercy from the five-year-old, but Bev came back with their food and saved him.

"Can I get you anything, Sheriff?" Bev asked.

He shook his head. "No thanks." After she walked away, Josiah turned toward Dean. "So it looks like you've only got the small trailer out there. Would you like some help unloading? I can meet you at your place at six. Melanie and I were already planning on stopping by, but I figured I'd double check with you first."

"I appreciate it," Dean said after finishing a bite of his cheeseburger. "We're going to head to the house after we're done eating and get started, but any time you can stop by and help would be great."

Nodding, Josiah looked over at Maya. "Are you excited to set up your new room?"

Silence.

"Maya," Dean said, his voice low but firm. "Sheriff Stone is talking to you."

She looked up at him defiantly and then looked over at Josiah. "I was more excited to go see Abby's ballet class. But Uncle Dean says we can't today."

"Ah…" Josiah said and then paused for a moment. He turned to Dean. "You're going to have extra hands helping you once I get off work so why don't you…"

Dean simply nodded and took another bite of his burger. "Sure. Thanks."

Standing, Josiah wished them both a good afternoon and waved as he walked away. "See you both around six!"

Dean waited until both he and Maya were almost done with their meals before speaking. "Since Josiah and Melanie are going to come help us out, we can go and see Abby. But…"

"We can?" she cried excitedly, all traces of sadness completely gone. "Yeah!"

"But…" he quickly interrupted, "we can only stay for thirty minutes. Understand?"

She nodded vigorously and took a long sip of her milkshake.

"So when I say it's time to go, I don't want any argument about it. Okay?"

Straw still in her mouth, she nodded again.

"I need you to promise, Maya," he said firmly – mainly because he had a feeling that she was testing his boundaries. And then he almost cringed at that thought. Damn parenting websites. He had been reading up on parenting ever since he went to Pennsylvania and found out that he was Maya's guardian. He read a ton of articles on the child's art of manipulation. It was hard to believe that someone so young could actually pull it off, but then again, it was also hard to believe how she went from bubbly and vivacious to sullen and weepy and then back again as soon as she got her way. He'd heard of this technique and how kids use it to wrap their parents around their little fingers.

Inwardly he sighed. There was going to be a whole hell of a lot of trial and error and it was going to go on for a while. He just knew it.

Across from him, Maya finished off her milkshake and looked at him with her sweetest smile. "You're the best uncle in the whole wide world!"

Yeah…he was a goner.

\*\*\*\*

Abby was doing warm-ups with her group when a movement by the door caught her eye. She smiled broadly when she spotted Dean and Maya and motioned for them to take a seat in the corner where the other parents were sitting. Doing her best not to focus on Dean being in the room – or how rugged and sexy he looked – Abby turned and helped the group go through the next three positions.

"Great job, everyone! Now let's step into the middle here and line up like we've been practicing," Abby called out and then walked toward Maya while her students got ready. "If you'd like to come and join us, you are more than welcome to."

Maya's eyes went wide. "Really?" she whispered loudly. "But I don't have the right shoes. Or anything."

Abby stood and held out her hand. "That's okay. I just want you to stand by me and watch what the girls are doing and see what you think." When Maya took her hand, Abby gave her another smile. "And it's completely okay if you just want to observe and not do any of the steps, so I don't want you to worry."

Nodding, Maya quietly followed Abby and then stood next to her as she called the class to order.

"Everyone, this is my friend Maya and she's here to observe our class today," Abby told the girls. "She's going to be standing by me so I don't want you to get too distracted. Stay focused on what you're doing and remember to look straight ahead and not at the floor." Using the remote for the music, she positioned herself so she could see everyone.

"We're going to start with the routine we performed at the fall festival and then we're going to start learning some new moves for our Christmas play. Is everyone ready?"

There was a collective round of yesses and then everyone took their positions. Abby clicked on the music and then stepped back to watch her girls dance. They were sweet and enthusiastic and while not completely graceful and coordinated, she was beyond proud of them. Sometimes one would leap left while everyone went right and then there was the occasional overly-enthusiastic spin that would make someone dizzy and end in a minor collision. Everyone took it in stride.

Standing beside Abby, Maya was simply swaying and watching every move the class made. Abby could tell that it was almost painful for the little girl to be still but she was incredibly impressed with her restraint. It was almost as if she didn't want to make a move until she had a clear understanding of how everything was supposed to go.

The music ended and everyone held their poses.

Abby broke the silence with a loud clap and the parents all joined in the applause. She had trained the girls not to get distracted and to simply take a small bow, then move into their positions for the next dance.

"That was wonderful," she said and began walking in front of the group. "I want everyone to line up the same way again and let me see how you look." Abby studied the girls. It was easy to see who had a growth spurt and would need to be moved while also taking into consideration who was struggling with being in the front. Within minutes, she made some minor adjustments and was pleased with the results.

Then she glanced over at Maya.

This would be Maya's class and if she did end up joining, Abby was going to need to make adjustments – better to do that now rather than once the girls were comfortable in their positions.

"Maya? Can you join me and the girls over here?"

Nodding, Maya joined her and soon enough, she had the perfect formation. Abby felt slightly bad for her new student – she certainly didn't fit in with her blue jeans and sneakers while the rest of the girls wore pink leotards, tights and tutus. For one day, though, she figured it would be all right. For the most part, Maya was so busy studying everyone's poses that she didn't seem to notice.

For the next thirty minutes, she slowly walked the group through the new steps and movements of their dance to "Winter Wonderland." Last year they had gone with "Silver Bells" but Abby felt it was important to keep their routines fresh. The beauty of the beginners' class was that the steps were all fairly simple. Either way, the students, parents and the town loved it.

The thought of getting to teach a more intensive ballet class to older students was really what Abby hoped to do eventually. Maybe if things worked out…

"Abby! Heather stepped on my toe!" little Dana Miller called out.

"I have to use the bathroom!" Ava Brady cried.

"Are we going to have angel wings?" Kristy Davis asked.

The music had stopped and it was clear that their attention span did as well. Clapping her hands together, she called out, "Okay! Good work today! I'm very proud of all of you. I want you to practice these new steps and be ready to move on next week." She paused. "Dana? I'm sure Heather didn't mean to step on your toe. Kristy? We haven't designed the costumes yet but I don't think we'll have wings this time. And Ava? You may go and use the bathroom. Class dismissed!"

There was instant scurrying around the room as the girls ran to their mothers – or to the restroom – and everyone began talking at once. Abby took a few minutes to let the room clear out a bit – mainly killing time until she could talk to Dean about Maya joining the class. It didn't take long and they actually walked across the room to approach her first.

She immediately smiled down at Maya. "So? What did you think?"

"I loved it! I want to be in your class! Did you see how I learned the steps? Did you see that I didn't fall?"

Chuckling, Abby nodded. "You did a great job." Then she looked up at Dean and saw that he looked a little…overwhelmed? Exhausted? Both. "So what did you think?" she asked him.

"Uh…" He looked down at Maya and then at Abby before focusing on his niece again. "Why don't you go get some water and let me talk to Abby for a minute, okay?"

She nodded and they both watched as she danced across the room toward the water fountain. "She's certainly enthusiastic."

Nodding, Dean faced her and sighed. "I really appreciate you letting her participate today. That meant a lot to her."

"I was happy to do it."

"The thing is…I just don't know how I'm going to do all of this yet," he said quietly, his voice a little low and gruff. "I realize you and I don't really know each other very well but…Maya's mother…my sister…"

Reaching out, Abby put a hand on his arm to stop him. "Small town," she said quietly. "And I think it's wonderful that Maya has you."

He nodded again. "Thanks." Raking a hand through his hair, he continued. "I have to get her registered for school and settled in and…it all just seems so overwhelming. And on top of all of that, I have a job. I haven't figured out how to handle her school schedule and my work schedule. From what I remember, there used to be afterschool programs for kids whose parents worked. I'm hoping that's still the case. And that would mean she couldn't get here for classes."

Abby knew he was right and yet…she looked over and saw Maya practicing her first position in front of the mirror. The little girl's face was serious and it was obvious she was determined to master the pose.

She looked back and Dean and hoped she wouldn't scare him with what she was about to say. "What if I were Maya's afterschool caregiver?" Before he could respond, she quickly went on. "I mean, like you said, we really don't know each other, but I know that you have a lot on your plate just from the little bit you shared with me. You can see how much Maya wants to dance and even though I don't have classes for her age group every day, I think she would get a kick out of hanging out here with me and watching the other classes." She paused and waited for him to respond. When he didn't, she added, "And on the days that I don't have classes I can still watch her. I'll pick her up at the bus stop and bring her to my place and you can pick her up after work."

He was staring at her as if she'd lost her mind.

It took a full minute for Dean to finally speak and when he did, his voice was full of uncertainty and hesitation. "I…why would you want to do that?"

Shrugging, Abby gave him a sheepish grin. "I love her enthusiasm and I believe in helping out a friend."

"We're not…I mean…we don't…" He seemed completely at a loss for words.

Her smile grew. "Everyone could use some new friends, right? So what do you say?"

He shook his head and sighed. For a minute, Abby was certain that he was going to turn her down but then Maya called out to show that she had indeed mastered first and second position and did the first three movements of the Christmas dance.

Abby saw Dean swallow hard before he faced her again. "I guess I say thank you and ask when you can start."

****

Maya chatted the entire way home and it was a welcome distraction. She sounded happy and he knew that – for now – it was all he could ask for. They had so much to do when they got to his house and just thinking about it was enough to freak him out.

Pulling into his driveway, he spotted Josiah's truck.

And several other cars.

*What the...?*

It was not even close to six o'clock. What was going on? He parked and helped Maya out and then walked up the front steps. The front door was slightly ajar and he heard voices. Walking in, Dean froze.

People were in his kitchen and from the sound of it, Josiah and a few other people were down the hall by the bedrooms.

"Uncle Dean? Who's here?"

"Um…some friends," he said distractedly.

Melanie – Josiah's fiancé – came out of the kitchen with a big smile on her face. "Hey! Welcome home!" She gave Dean a hug and then crouched down and introduced herself to Maya.

"Um…what's going on?" he asked.

She stood up and – if possible – smiled even brighter. "Come see!"

In his kitchen was Bev from the diner, Erika from the bookstore, Nikki from the ice cream parlor, along with Shari and Danielle from Doc McGuire's office. "Surprise!" they cried, all smiling. They all were talking at once but from what Dean could tell, they had food shopped for him and prepared enough meals to get him and Maya through at least a week.

"I…I don't know what to say," he stammered, truly humbled by their thoughtfulness. This was more people than he'd ever had in his home and it was a little disconcerting.

"But that's not all," Melanie said, motioning for them to follow her down the hall. "I really hope you don't mind that we took the initiative here, but…"

They stopped at the door to his guest room and beside him, Maya gasped. "Is this my room?"

"It sure is!" Melanie said. "I hope you like princesses!"

Maya nodded enthusiastically. "I do! I do! I really do!"

Dean stared in awe at the transformation. When he'd left for Pennsylvania two weeks ago, this room had bare walls that were painted a dingy white. There was no furniture or carpeting in that room and it held boxes and stuff that he just didn't feel inclined to put into storage.

But now?  Now there were pink walls and crisp white trim and curtains on the windows.  He stepped further into the room and marveled at the artwork on the walls of several Disney princesses and the pink chandelier that hung from the ceiling.

He looked over at Josiah and…words escaped him.

As if sensing that, his friend walked over and clapped him on the shoulder.  "We thought you could use a hand.  I didn't want to say anything to you because I knew you'd try to talk me out of it and tell me that you didn't want – or need – the help. But now, well…it's just a few less things for you to think about."

"I…I'm overwhelmed," Dean said, his voice thick with emotion.  Looking around the room he saw several of his friends standing there smiling, being supportive.  "The whole ride home I thought about how much work it was going to take to give Maya a room that would make her feel at home and…and…"

"I know you'd do the same for me," Josiah said quietly.  After a quiet moment, he called out to everyone.  "Now let's get the trailer unloaded so these two can settle in."  Then he looked at Dean and smiled.  "Pizza's on the way too."

And in that moment, Dean was incredibly grateful for the community of Silver Bell Falls.  It felt good to be home.

# Three

It was Maya's first day of school and Dean was already exhausted. Thinking about the long supplies list Maya's teacher had handed him and the fact that it was only two weeks until Thanksgiving had Dean questioning how he was going to survive.

After his conversation with Abby on Thursday, they arranged for Maya to stay with her after school. The plan had been for Dean to pick his niece up before six. Looking at the clock, he saw it was after seven and he groaned. True, he'd texted Abby and let her know he'd been detained at work, but this certainly wasn't the best way to start off this arrangement.

And there was still the school supplies shopping list and dinner and probably homework to get through.

How did people – parents – do this? He wondered, not for the first time today. And single parents in particular. It was as if you had to be at least two different people! No, make that three. You had to be mother and father and then you had to be yourself – the person who works and pays the bills and tries their best to hold onto their sanity.

Dean knew he was losing that battle for sure.

Pulling into Abby's driveway, he felt himself sag with relief. He was here. Finally. And somehow, they'd get everything done. Maybe it wasn't the best or the most organized way, but he'd be damn sure that Maya's needs were met.

And then he would fall into bed and sleep.

And it would be glorious.

Wearily, he made his way up the front steps of Abby's home and swore he could hear music and…laughing. There was a large picture window to the right of the doorway and he took a chance and stepped over to see if he could see inside. The sight before him made Dean feel like his heart was squeezing.

Abby was doing some sort of…spin. Twirl. Something. One leg was straight out in front of her and she was going around and around and around. Beside her, Maya was doing her best to mimic the move and she was smiling and laughing and…he sighed happily. She looked like a happy, carefree child rather than one who'd just lost her mom and had her entire life uprooted. She had on a pink leotard, ballet slippers and a tutu. Dean frowned slightly because he knew he hadn't had a chance to purchase any of that yet. Maybe Abby had extras and lent them to Maya.

Deciding he was late enough, he stepped back over and rang the doorbell. The music instantly went off and before he knew it, Abby was opening the door with a smile on her face.

"Hey," she said. "Come on in."

Was her voice always that soft? Husky? He wondered. Clearing his throat, he thanked her and walked in.

"Uncle Dean! Look! Look!" Maya cried as she ran over to him. She stopped right in front of him and then spun around. "Look at my tutu! And my tights! And my leotard! And the slippers! I got everything!"

Crouching down, he smiled at her. "You sure did and you look just like a ballerina." It was clearly the perfect thing to say because her entire face lit up with joy. "Did Abby lend these to you?"

Maya shook her head. "Uh-uh. She gave them to me! As a present!"

Dean made sure to keep his smile in place even as he glanced up at Abby. She blushed and immediately began moving around the living room picking up what he assumed were some of Maya's things.

"A present, huh?" he asked his niece. "That was very nice of her."

Maya nodded. "She said it was to welcome me to Silver Bell Falls!"

"Maya, why don't you go and get changed back into your clothes and then we'll get your school stuff packed up, okay?" Abby asked.

"But I want to stay in my ballerina clothes! Can I? Please?"

Dean was about to tell her that it wasn't polite to argue, but Abby stepped over and responded like a pro.

"Our dance uniforms are just for that – dancing. If you wear them all the time, they won't last as long and you risk spilling something on them and ruining them." She paused and smiled as Maya seemed to be contemplating her words. "And you don't want to ruin these already, do you?"

"No," Maya said, her tone serious. "They're too pretty. I'm gonna go change." And just like that, she scampered off.

Dean stood as soon as Maya was out of the room. Facing Abby, he slid his hands into his pockets and smiled. "I'm impressed."

She looked at him quizzically. "With what?"

"You got her to do what you wanted to do – even though she didn't want to. How did you do that?"

"Ah," Abby said, chuckling. "She's going to be testing her boundaries with you for a while, I'm sure. But I'm not a parental figure, so I have it a little easier." She turned and walked into the kitchen. Dean followed.

"So…um…how much do I owe you for the dance clothes?"

Without looking at him, Abby grabbed some potholders and opened the oven. Pulling out a covered roasting dish, she placed it on the counter before responding to him. "You don't owe me anything, Dean. Like Maya said, they were a gift."

"Abby," he said softly, not wanting Maya to overhear them, "You're already doing enough for us. You helped me out today and I'm sorry that I got here so late. I'm sure you have your own life to live and it looks like we held up your dinner." He muttered a curse. "We're not off to a very good start, are we?"

She considered him for a moment and motioned toward her kitchen table. "Why don't you have a seat?" Dean did as she requested. "Can I get you something to drink?"

He shook his head. "We really should be going. I still have school supplies to get and dinner to make." Hanging his head, he shook it again. "It's going to get easier, right?" Dean heard the desperation in his voice and hated it.

Abby didn't answer. Instead she moved around the kitchen and it took a minute for him to realize that the table was set for three and that...*wait a minute*. "Did you make dinner for us?" he asked incredulously.

Taking the seat beside him, Abby leaned in close to him. "Look," she began quietly, "I grew up with a single mom. I know how hard it is. And yes, it's going to get easier. But it's going to take time. So if I can help, I'm going to."

"Abby," he said, surprising himself when he reached out and covered her hand with his, "I'm never going to learn if I never have to do anything. I can't rely on you to take care of it all."

Her smile was sweet and compassionate and…damn but her eyes were green, he thought. Why hadn't he noticed that before? As a matter of fact, why hadn't he noticed a lot of things about Abby before? He'd eaten at the diner enough that he knew a little about her – like that she was sweet and friendly and pretty. Dammit, he knew he was staring but he couldn't seem to make himself look away. She was beautiful.

Breathtaking, really.

"I'm not taking care of it all," she replied, interrupting his thoughts. "I'm merely helping you get your bearings."

"Abby…"

Slowly, she pulled her hand from his and stood up. "Okay, so the ballet clothes were a gift because Maya was going to need them for class today. I wanted her to feel good and fit in. And dinner because…well…I knew you were going to be late and I thought it would be nice. It's not good to eat dinner late, especially for a child. And the school supplies…"

"Wait…you bought her school supplies?" he asked, a hint of indignation in his voice.

Unfazed, Abby began making their plates. "I did. After class, I had to go and look at something and we went to the store and got some supplies because Maya mentioned that she had homework. She was worried that she didn't have the right paper or crayons so…" She shrugged. "It wasn't a big deal."

He jumped up and stalked over to her. "Well it's a big deal to me! A very big deal! I know I got behind today, but that doesn't mean I don't know what I'm doing or that…that…I need someone bailing me out! Maya's my responsibility, not yours, and I can damn well go and get her school supplies if she needs them!"

As soon as the words were out of his mouth, he realized he was overreacting. The correct response would have been to thank her – she helped him out and he needed it. Raking a hand through his hair, he moved away and paced a little.

"I'm sorry," he said gruffly. "I guess…this is all just overwhelming."

Amazingly enough, Abby didn't seem to be bothered at all by his outburst. "How about I'll let you bail me out when I'm overwhelmed the next time?"

Dean noticed the smirk on her face and couldn't help but smile. "Now you're making fun of me."

She laughed softly. "Maybe. Just a little."

Clearing his throat, Dean relaxed a bit. "What did you have to go look at?"

Abby looked over her shoulder at him as she continued to make up their plates, confusion on her face.

"You mentioned going to look at something after class. What was it?"

Her shoulders sagged a little as she turned back to their dinner plates. "I'm trying to find a place for a real dance studio.  Millie Taylor's helping and today I went and looked at a building over on Second Avenue."

"Was it any good?"

She shook her head.  "I'm telling you –I don't think I'm asking for much, but I can't seem to find a building anywhere in Silver Bell that meets my criteria "  She sighed  "Maybe I'm just being too picky."

"I find that hard to believe."

With a shrug, she turned and began moving their plates to the table.  She called out to Maya and within minutes the three of them were seated around the table.

"Uncle Dean, I helped Abby with dinner!  I put the carrots and potatoes in the pan and Abby said I did a great job!"

And there it was again, that squeeze around his heart.

"…but Abby did all the work with the chicken," Maya continued.  "I thought it felt weird and I didn't want to touch it.  But Abby said it was okay."

Looking over at Dean, Abby smiled.  "I hope you like chicken."

"I love it and I love it even more when I don't have to cook it.  Or when it's not in a casserole," he said with a wink.

"Ah…you got a bunch of food brought over, I take it," she said.

"How did you know?"

Abby chuckled. "I work with Bev and she heads up the committee. Whenever there's a family in need, there's a group of ladies who make food – casseroles – and bring them over. It's kind of sweet, really." Then she paused. "Unless you don't like casseroles."

"I actually enjoy them…"

"But…" she prompted.

"But…I'm ready for something that's not a casserole."

"Can we say grace?" Maya asked. Both adults looked at her. "My friend Molly – she lives back where I used to live – she always says grace when her family sits down to have dinner. And we're like a family right now, so can we say it too?"

If Dean thought his heart was squeezing before, he couldn't quite breathe now. He couldn't speak if he wanted to and was thankful when Abby responded, saying "That would be very nice". Then she reached out and took one of Dean's hands and then one of Maya's.

"Why don't you say it tonight, Maya?" Abby prompted.

He listened as his niece thanked God for him and Abby, her new school and new friends before asking God to give her mom a kiss for her. She thanked God for their food and for her new ballet clothes. She paused and Dean was certain that she was done, but then she added one last thing.

"And thank you, God, for finally giving me a family to have dinner with like all my friends. Amen."

Right then and there, Dean wasn't sure he'd be able to eat a bite of his dinner. Not with the lump of emotion clogging his throat.

**\*\*\*\***

It was after eleven and Abby was lying in bed staring at the ceiling.

*What in the world have I done?* She wondered – and not for the first time tonight.

Offering to help Dean with Maya was a no-brainer, and not because she'd been crushing on Dean for a while. Okay, maybe "a while" was too vague, she thought. The truth was that she'd been crushing on Dean for well over a year. Ever since she took the job at the diner and saw him for breakfast most days, she was hooked.

He'd always been polite and quiet and never expressed any interest in her whatsoever, but that hadn't stopped Abby from being hopeful.

And it still wasn't the reason for her offer to help with Maya.

She'd told him the truth earlier – she had grown up with a single parent and always remembered how hard her mom worked and how overwhelmed she was and…well…she hated to see anyone else struggle like that. Dean's circumstances added to that. Dean Hayes, bachelor and all-around recluse, was suddenly thrust into the role of guardian. Parent. That would have to be hard for anyone, but she had a feeling it was particularly hard for Dean since he lived such a solitary life.

And on top of it, she simply fell in love with Maya. Her big blue eyes and those blonde ringlets gave her an angelic look. But most of all, it had been Maya's talking about dance that pulled Abby's heartstrings. Back when she was little, it had been a hardship for her to take dance classes. She could still remember the day her mother sat her down and said she was going to work an extra job cleaning the dance studio two towns over just so Abby could take classes there.

Even thinking about it still had her tearing up. It had been a huge sacrifice. Her mother had already been working two jobs. The cleaning job was the most physically demanding one, but it was downright brutal after already working fifty hours a week. When Abby got older, she helped her mom with the cleaning. Some of the other dancers made fun of her and called her names because of their poor lifestyle, but it taught Abby the value of working for something you love.

Dancing came easy to her and while she hadn't been accepted to Julliard, Abby received a scholarship to the College of Performing Arts in Pennsylvania. She went for four years and did some traveling with a dance company for several years after graduation. After a while, Abby realized she was homesick and just wanted to be back in Silver Bell.

Working as a waitress wasn't her dream but she came back with the hope of teaching dance and starting up her own studio.

It was just taking longer than she'd expected.

She had friends who thought she was crazy to leave the performing world behind, but Abby didn't regret it. She was looking to the future and knew that this was where she was meant to be. And after meeting Maya it simply confirmed that she could make a difference. She wanted to – needed to – share her gift, her talents, with her students. It was an amazing thing to watch the joy on someone's face as they mastered a dance. It made Abby feel good knowing that she was playing a part in making someone else's dreams come true.

Maya needed her.

Dean needed her. Even if he didn't want to admit it or if he didn't like it.

Maya's dinner prayer of thanks had been heartbreaking. This small child had her life turned upside down and she was grasping for some sense of normalcy. The last thing Abby wanted to do was give her false hope, but if having dinner together made her feel good, then so be it.

The look of shock and sadness on Dean's face had been heartbreaking in its own right. For the life of her, Abby couldn't even begin to imagine what must be going through his mind. When he'd shown up tonight he looked tired and frazzled and completely unsure of himself. He didn't have any family left here and although they hadn't talked about it, she had to wonder where his parents were and why they weren't helping out with Maya's care until she got settled.

A conversation for another time, she supposed. In the meantime, Abby knew she'd continue to do what she could to help this new little family out.

They were helping her out as well. It had been nice to cook dinner for someone other than herself and it had been fun to leap around the house and dance with someone who loved it as much as she did.

They might not be a real family, but they certainly filled voids in each other's lives.

At least for right now.

She just hoped that she didn't get too attached, too dependent on them. Dean had already expressed his displeasure with her doing so much for them, but he had no idea that some of her motives were selfish.

She missed out on having a family.

It had always been just Abby and her mom. When her mom retired and moved to Arizona three years ago, Abby learned just how big of a hole one person could leave in your life.

Tonight that hole was filled by two amazing people. And maybe – just maybe – she filled one for them too.

Rolling over, she yawned and snuggled beneath her flannel sheets.

They'd make a nice little family…

**\*\*\*\***

They'd made it through their first week.

It was five-forty-five and Dean was pulling into the community center's parking lot and feeling pretty good about it. He was caught up on his work and found a way to get things done so that he could see Maya get on the bus in the morning and then be at Abby's before dinnertime.

Not that he hadn't enjoyed eating with her Monday night. He had. A lot. More than he thought he could. After hearing Maya's prayer before they ate, he realized how impressionable she was and didn't want to do anything else to confuse her so he'd been extra conscientious about getting into a routine where they ate dinner – just the two of them – at home.

From what Dean knew of Abby's schedule, today's class was for students who were a little older than Maya. He knew she didn't mind having Maya there during the class, but he had a feeling that there were going to be times when his niece was going to be a distraction. Maybe not intentionally, but it was certain to happen.

Walking into the community center, he waved to Kathy Jones who manned the information desk as he made his way toward the dance room. He could hear the music and wondered if Abby would be dancing or just observing. Ballet was never anything that even remotely interested Dean, yet watching Abby dance was becoming a favorite pastime.

Actually, just watching Abby move in general was becoming a favorite pastime.

Not that he wanted to think about that right now. He did enough of that late at night when he was finally alone. He would close his eyes and there she was - in his mind - dancing. Moving. Just...being Abby.

That had the potential to be a major complication in this whole situation and Dean refused to let that happen. He needed to focus on Maya and getting her settled and making sure she was happy and all of her needs were met. That's what was most important. The fact that he was suddenly attracted - *distracted* - by a woman just happened to be poor timing on his part.

Stepping into the doorway of the dance room, he froze.

Abby was dancing.

Quietly, he slid in and onto the edge of the chair that was right next to the door. And then he just...watched. She was so elegant, so graceful and when she moved it was like...her body was so fluid. She made every leap, every turn, every...everything look effortless. The class wasn't dancing with her. They were simply watching - enthralled, just as he was. Dean spotted Maya sitting against the far wall watching Abby with awe.

Yeah. He knew the feeling.

The music stopped and Abby stood completely still in the middle of the room. She wasn't even breathing hard. Dean was practically panting and felt like his breath was echoing off the walls. Did he clap? Stand up and cheer? Seriously, he had no idea what he was supposed to do after watching such a performance but sitting here silently just felt wrong. Clearly her class felt the same way because they all jumped up and started clapping. Unable to help himself, he joined in.

Abby smiled as she turned and thanked all of them - accepting their praise and hugs as she made her way to the corner of the room to grab her bottle of water. She took a long drink before calling them all to attention.

"Okay, next week we're going to move on to our next series of moves for your Christmas performance. I need you to make sure that you practice and that you bring your checks for your costumes with you. Shelly Stallings will be taking your measurements next Friday and if you aren't going to be here, you'll need to have your moms let me know so we can make arrangements for you to get them done." She paused. "Have a great weekend!"

Dean stepped farther into the room and away from the doorway to make room for the students and parents who were leaving. He waved to some, said a quick hello to others, but he was anxious to get to Maya and head home. They were going to eat the last of the casseroles tonight and tomorrow they would tackle food shopping so he could finally stock the house with things that they both liked and then next week he'd have to get into the habit of coming home and making dinner.

Not that he didn't eat dinner before Maya came to live with him, but it was just a lot more…laid back. Casual. And there was never a designated dinner time. This was going to take a lot of getting used to.

Just like everything else had been in the last few weeks.

"Uncle Dean!" Maya ran over and jumped into his arms. She was finally comfortable with him and if he didn't know any better, he'd say she was starved for affection. She was always hugging him or holding his hand and…it felt good. Nice. Dean hadn't realized it but that was something that had been missing from his life too.

And now they had each other.

"Well there are two of my favorite people," Abby said as she walked over. Today she was wearing a black leotard and tights and had some sort of sheer short skirt wrapped around her. Every inch of her body clearly defined by the clingy material and it was hard for him to tear his gaze away. The classroom was empty but for the three of them and as she stepped closer, Dean noticed that she looked a little tired. "Any exciting plans this weekend?"

"We're eating the last of the casseroles tonight," Maya announced. "And Uncle Dean said tomorrow we get to go and pick out all our own food!"

Abby looked at him and laughed softly. "That is exciting!"

Dean couldn't help but laugh with her. "Trust me, I never thought I'd look forward to a trip to the supermarket, but right now I really do."

"Well good for the two of you!" She looked down at Maya. "What's your favorite snack?"

"Cookies!"

"Ooh…mine too," Abby said. "Chocolate chip are my absolute favorite."

"Me too! They're the best!"

"And my favorite way to have them is when they are freshly baked and they're still warm and then have a big giant glass of milk with them," Abby said with glee. "So good!"

"You can eat warm chocolate chip cookies?" Maya asked, confused.

"Absolutely! They're easy to bake and then you take them out of the oven and let them cool for a few minutes and…"

"Uncle Dean? Can we bake cookies this weekend?"

"Uh…"

"Tell you what," Abby said quickly. "Once we get through all of the practices for the Christmas performance, we'll bake cookies together. What do you say?"

"I say yeah!" Maya cried. "But can we do it before Christmas? I bet Santa would like homemade cookies."

"I think you're right," Abby said with a wink. "We'll have a few days between the performance and Christmas Eve when we can make time to bake. Sound good?"

Maya nodded. "But now I gotta use the bathroom." She took off before anyone said anything else.

"It seems like the two of you are really settling in. I can see a difference in her already."

He nodded, sliding his hands into his pockets. "We are. It's not easy but…every day it gets a little less overwhelming."

"That's a good thing."

They stood in silence and Dean felt like he had so much that he wanted to say to her – to thank her for – but for the life of him, he couldn't make himself speak. She looked a little tired and yet…she was still breathtaking. He wanted to reach out and caress her cheek, run his fingers into her hair and shake it free of the tight bun in which she currently had it up. He wanted to massage her shoulders and do something for her because he had a feeling that the only person taking care of Abby was…Abby. He wanted to…

"Anyway," she said and took a step back before walking to the corner of the room, "next week we have fittings for the costumes for the Christmas play. So next Friday we'll be here a little late. I hope that's all right."

Nodding, he moved across the room toward her, still unsure of what to do or say.

"After Thanksgiving we'll have a couple of extra classes but I'll have a printout of the schedule for all the parents next week. So those Tuesdays where I normally just take Maya back to my house, I'll have her here with me."

He nodded again and watched as Abby pulled a bulky sweatshirt on over her leotard and then she gracefully wrapped a wool scarf around her neck. It was green – the color of her eyes. She bent over and…holy hell! Her body was…well, it was perfect. Dean's hands literally twitched with the need to touch her. When she straightened, he quickly looked away – certain she'd be able to tell what he was thinking.

Abby let out a little sigh and looked around the room. "I think that's everything." She smiled at him again. "I hope you guys have a great weekend. If you need anything, just…"

And that's when it hit him like a bolt of lightning. He did need something.

"Dean? Are you okay?"

"Huh? What?"

"Are you okay?" she repeated, taking a step closer to him. "You sort of zoned out there for a moment and had a strange look on your face."

Before he could second-guess himself or chicken out, he took a step closer – closing the gap between them.  "I'm fine," he said gruffly.  "But I need to do this."

And then he lowered his head and claimed her lips with his.

He had never been the impulsive type and yet right now, it seemed like the most logical thing in the world to kiss Abby.  And, by the way she was responding, the feeling was mutual.

Her arms wound around his shoulders as his went around her waist.  Hearing her sigh and feeling her melt against him was such an incredible feeling that he tightened his grip.  His tongue teased hers and he felt her hands rake up into his hair and…

"Why are you kissing Abby?"

They immediately broke apart.  Abby took a step back and turned away from him for a minute.  Dean looked at his niece's wide eyes and wondered what the hell he was thinking.  They weren't alone and kissing Abby in the middle of the community center wasn't the smartest thing to do – impulsive or not.

"Um…we were…we were just…" Dean stammered.

Maya's eyes narrowed a little.  "Do you like Abby?"

"Uh…yes," he replied honestly and had to keep his focus on Maya even as he heard Abby's soft gasp at his confession.  "I do.  I like Abby a lot."

Without a word, Maya walked across the room and went to pick up her backpack and her jacket.  When she turned and faced the two of them, her expression was serious. "Will I have to go sleep at the babysitter's now?"

Dean was confused for a minute. He looked over at Abby and she seemed just as lost as he was. He was just about to ask Maya what she meant, but as usual, she was one step ahead of him.

"Mommy used to send me to the babysitter's when she had a date. Sometimes she didn't come back for a couple of days."

Dean's heart broke. Her voice was trembling slightly and he could tell that she was afraid – afraid that she was going to be left behind again. There was no way he was going to let that happen but…there was also no way he wasn't going to explore this attraction with Abby. Maybe…

"Can Abby have dinner with us?"

"Um…what?" he asked.

Maya nodded and walked over to the two of them, suddenly looking like she had a solution. "Can Abby come home with us and have dinner? Maybe we can bake some cookies tonight and then after I go to bed, you can kiss her again. You know, if you want to."

"Oh…um…" Abby began.

"We could stop at the grocery store on the way home and find something to make that isn't a leftover casserole and get ingredients to make cookies," Dean suggested, his focus solely on Abby. When she looked at him, she blushed and it was a sexy look on her.

"I appreciate the offer, but I'm supposed to go and meet with a realtor to look at another building. Why don't we aim for tomorrow night? You guys pick out something to make for dinner and I'll bring the ingredients for the cookies. What do you think?"

Dean thought it sounded like he'd have to wait another twenty-four hours before kissing her again and it didn't sound appealing at all. Beside him, Maya was already chatting about what other kinds of cookies they could make beside the chocolate chip.

They all walked out of the community center together – waving to Kathy as they left - and by the time they were at their cars, he had resigned himself to the wait. He got Maya settled into her booster seat before turning to Abby.

"So…"

"So…" she repeated with a shy smile.

He stepped in close to her and was relieved that she didn't move away. "Should I apologize for kissing you earlier?"

Her head tilted as she studied him. "That depends."

"On what?"

"On whether or not you intend to do it again."

That was…cryptic. "So let's say I planned on kissing you again…that would mean…"

Abby laughed softly. "That would mean that no apology was necessary." She paused. "And just for the record, I'd be totally on board with you kissing me again."

Relief swamped him as he leaned in and placed a chaste kiss on her lips. When he pulled back, he gave her a sheepish grin. "I would love to do more but…"

"Understood," she said softly. "I guess I'll see you both tomorrow."

He nodded. "Have a good night, Abby." After she wished him one as well, he watched her walk away and thought about how this was a damn good night indeed.

# Four

Standing at Dean's front door the next night, Abby wondered – not for the first time – just what exactly she was doing.

Dean's kiss had shocked the hell out of her – but she recovered quickly. The man kissed better than her fantasies about him and if Maya hadn't interrupted them, she just might have wrapped herself around him completely and refused to let go.

Probably not a good thing.

This was an incredibly delicate and complicated situation. It wasn't just the two of them. Maya was a key factor and no matter how much Abby wanted to be with Dean, Maya's needs and well-being had to come first.

This would all be fairly easy to deal with if Dean hadn't been such a great kisser. Unfortunately, he was, and it was going to be a major distraction. Maybe she shouldn't have come. Or maybe she'd have to find an excuse to leave early. Or maybe…

"Are you gonna come inside?" Maya asked when she pulled the front door open. She was looking at Abby quizzically. "Uncle Dean said you were just standing out here and we should wait for you to ring the bell but I thought maybe you didn't know that we had a bell."

"I was just…um…I was standing here thinking that I hoped I remembered all the ingredients for the cookies," Abby said confidently and almost sagged with relief when Maya didn't question her. The kid certainly had a knack for being intuitive.

Stepping into the house, Abby went right to the kitchen and smiled at the sight of Dean stirring something on the stove. "Smells good," she said, placing her grocery bags down on the counter. "What are we having?"

"Spaghetti and meatballs. Maya said it's her favorite and that's pretty lucky because it's one of the few things I can make," Dean said to her, smiling and looking relaxed.

"I'm just going to put some of this…" Dean swooped in and kissed her soundly. When he lifted his head, she felt a little dizzy. "Wow."

"I know," he murmured and placed one more kiss on her cheek before moving away.

Her heart was beating a little erratically and she wanted to kick herself. How crazy was it that one little kiss in the middle of a kitchen could turn her so upside down? Crazy *and* pathetic, she chided herself. Maya popped up in front of her and broke her out of her mental dialogue.

"Is that all the ingredients for the cookies?" she asked anxiously.

"Sure is! We're going to make chocolate chip cookies and sugar cookies tonight. And we have colored sugar sprinkles to decorate the sugar cookies with."

"Really?" Maya asked. "Did you bring cookie cutters too?"

Damn. Why hadn't she thought of that? "Not this time. I thought for our first time baking we'd stick to regular round cookies. We'll go shopping and find some fun Christmas ones after Thanksgiving."

That seemed to satisfy her and for the next few minutes, they chatted about what it took to bake cookies while Dean quietly worked beside them getting their dinner ready. As Abby looked around the kitchen, she couldn't help but get caught up in the domesticity of it all. Here they were, all working together to put a meal and dessert together and really, it was a lot of fun. Maya's chatter filled any lull in the conversation but she had so much enthusiasm for everything she was saying that Abby couldn't help but get excited with her.

"So after we eat and clean up the dinner dishes, we'll spread out on the kitchen table with our baking sheets and rolling pins and get started," Abby was saying.

"How long will it take to make them?"

"I'd say it will take us about an hour before we'll have some cookies coming out of the oven. So that will give us plenty of time to relax and give our tummies a rest after this delicious dinner your uncle is making for us!"

"It's my favorite," Maya said proudly.

Beside her, Dean chuckled. "You also said that about cheeseburgers, strawberry milkshakes, pizza and the ham sandwich you had for lunch yesterday. You have a lot of favorites," he teased.

Nodding, Maya looked at Abby. "I really do. But they're all so good that I can't pick just one."

Chuckling, Abby nodded. "Can I help with anything?"

"You and Maya can set the table and everything here should be ready in about five minutes." They all worked together and – just as he'd said – they were sitting down at the table a few minutes later.

Over dinner, they talked about a dozen different topics – mostly initiated by Maya – that ranged from food to dancing to Christmas and her wish list. Abby was amazed that her list wasn't longer – most kids had about a dozen different things on it, but Maya's list had been short and precise.

A second set of ballet clothes.

A new coat.

And a doll that was a ballerina.

Both Abby and Dean were silent for a moment and before Abby could even comment on her list, Maya was talking again.

"I saw one that had a red ballet dress and one that wears all pink like we do for our classes. Either one of those would be great. I've got my list all ready to send to Santa." She looked at Dean. "Can you put it in the mail for me?"

He nodded. "Of course. You know, we could go to the mall tomorrow and see Santa in person and then you can give him the letter yourself."

Her eyes went wide. "Really? We can see Santa in person?"

Abby sat there in disbelief. What had Maya's young life been like before her mother died? It seemed like so many things that most people take for granted – baking cookies or sitting on Santa's lap – were completely foreign to her! There was no way she could say anything – especially not right now – and maybe it wasn't polite to ask Dean what the hell was wrong with his sister, but…that's exactly what Abby was thinking!

Dean looked over at her and it was like he could read her mind. The look he gave her said that he was equally offended and she had no choice but to force herself to calm down.

The rest of the dinner was fairly pleasant and then they all worked together to clean up so they could start working on the cookies. Abby had to say, it was a lot messier when you were doing it with an enthusiastic child. Dean wasn't taking part in baking, but he was certainly busy cleaning up around Maya who'd dropped flour and sugar and was almost covered in it herself.

When they were ready to put the first two pans in the oven, Abby had a suggestion. "Tell you what, Maya Papaya…why don't you go and take a super quick shower while these bake so you'll be all clean when we're ready to eat them? Can you do that?"

Her response was a very exuberant "Yes!" right before she ran from the room.

Dean chuckled. "That was brilliant thinking," he said. "I'll be back in a few. I need to get her set up in there and make sure she has a towel and clean pajamas with her."

"Take your time. We have twelve minutes of baking but I'll wait five minutes before putting them in to give her a little extra time. I don't want Maya to miss seeing them come out of the oven."

Without a word, Dean walked over to her and kissed her gently on the lips before turning to go help Maya.

Abby thought to herself that she would have to start coming up with plenty of brilliant ideas if her reward was a kiss from Dean.

****

Maya was so excited about the cookies that she didn't argue with him at all about taking a shower. Normally she preferred a bath but tonight, she was all about getting clean quickly. He turned on the water in the shower, got her clean pajamas and a towel and then helped her in. He didn't go far because he knew she'd need help washing her hair – something that he was learning to do for her.

All in all, it only took about ten minutes and she chatted the entire time about the cookies – retelling him everything she and Abby did to make them. Who would have thought that baking cookies could make such an impression?

Quickly drying her off, he helped her into her pajamas and quickly combed her hair; with its natural curliness, there wasn't much to do with it except let it dry on its own. When they walked back into the kitchen, Dean saw that Abby had cleaned up some more and she smiled when she spotted them.

Damn. He really did enjoy looking at her and seeing her in his home, his kitchen. It just felt…right.

"Are you ready to take the cookies out?" Abby asked.

"Yes! Yes! Yes!" Maya cried as she jumped up and down. "Are you sure they're done? How long will it take for them to cool off? How many am I allowed to eat?"

"One question at a time, Maya," Dean commented. Then he simply stood back and let the two of them work together to take the pans out of the oven. Abby had on the oven mitts and when she pulled out the first tray, she held it so that Maya could see how the cookies looked and how you could tell that they were done. She placed the tray down on top of the stove and then pulled out the second sheet and placed it beside it.

"I have special racks that we use to help the cookies cool. These pans are very hot so I don't want you to get too close to them. I'll move the cookies to the racks and then we'll get ready to put the next batch in the oven, okay?"

Maya nodded and watched as Abby did what she'd just explained. Ten minutes later, the next batch of cookies were going in the oven. That was the last of the cookie dough and while that batch baked, Abby and Maya worked together to clean up the kitchen. Dean had offered to help, but Abby told him that it was important for Maya to learn the importance of cleaning up. Surprisingly, his niece didn't argue.

The kitchen was clean, the entire house smelled of freshly baked cookies and Dean felt happier than he had in a long time. Maybe his father had been right; maybe he and Maya really did need each other. Life had certainly gotten a lot more demanding but…he was beginning to see all of the unexpected benefits to that. Besides the bonding he and Maya were doing, Dean was getting involved in the community more and…he had Abby.

Well, he didn't *have* her. Not like that. Not yet anyway. But…he was really enjoying their time together and was anxious to see where it was all going to lead.

"Uncle Dean, are you going to have milk with your cookies too?"

He chuckled. "Of course! You can't have cookies without milk!"

That seemed to please her and she worked with Abby to get another glass down from the cabinet and then went and got the milk from the refrigerator. In minutes, they were all seated around the table and enjoying warm, freshly-baked cookies.

Dean noticed the anxious look on Abby's face as she watched Maya.

"So?" she asked. "What do you think? Do you like warm cookies?"

Maya nodded her head vigorously. "These are the best cookies! I love them like this! They are my favorite!"

"Uh-oh," Dean said dramatically. "Another favorite food? How am I supposed to keep up with this?"

Maya giggled uncontrollably at his comment and Dean had to admit, he loved the sound of her laughter. Soon they were all laughing and that was even better. For far too long his house had been quiet. Empty. Almost void of life. And now? Here he was sitting at the kitchen table with two amazing females who made him happy. How great of a gift was that?

Once their laughter died down, they finished eating the cookies – not all of the cookies, just the amount that Abby had plated for them. It was late, almost nine o'clock, which was Maya's bedtime.  She thanked Abby for teaching her to bake cookies and then kissed her goodnight.  Dean picked her up and carried her down the hall to her room.

"Do you want a story tonight?" he asked.

"Can Abby read one to me?"

"We can ask," he said, placing her down on the bed. "Why don't you pick a book and I'll go ask her?"

"Okay!"

Walking back to the kitchen, he saw Abby cleaning up again.  "You know you don't have to keep doing that. It was already pretty clean in here."

Abby shrugged and smiled at him.  "I needed something to do while you got Maya ready for bed.  Is she asleep already?"

Dean couldn't help but laugh.  "That would be something," he teased.  "Actually, she wanted to know if you'd read her a story tonight.  We've been doing that almost every night and so…"

"I would love to," she replied, quickly drying her hands.  Walking down to Maya's room, Dean watched as Abby sat down on the bed and took the book his niece had picked out and smiled.

He stood in the doorway quietly and just watched and listened.  A month ago, he never could have imagined this being his life.  He had no idea that he'd be enjoying the sound of a child's laugh or listening to a beautiful woman read a children's book, and yet…here he was.

He understood now. The things he couldn't wrap his brain around while dealing with his parents back in Pennsylvania, it all made sense now. It would have been the wrong decision for them to take Maya. She needed a lot of attention and she had boundless energy and really, she needed someone who needed and wanted her. Sometimes it was hard to understand why life handed you some of the curves that it did and sometimes you were lucky enough to get that understanding and have peace with it.

Making a mental note to call his parents the next day, he noticed that Maya was asleep – and Abby was barely at the halfway point in the book. He gave her a thumbs up and watched as she gingerly climbed from the bed and walked quietly across the room to him.

"I can't believe she fell asleep so fast," she whispered.

"She has two speeds – full throttle and out cold," Dean said quietly. Reaching for Abby's hand, he turned out the light and led her out of the room and to the living room. "Can I get you something to drink?"

She shook her head. "I'm fine, thanks."

They sat down and for a moment, simply enjoyed the quiet.

"Thank you for all that you did tonight," he finally said. "I'm sure you could tell how much it meant to

Maya. And to me. I guess…sometimes it's hard for me to understand how much she's missed out on because my sister…" He stopped and shook his head. He didn't want to go there.

"Like I've said before, I grew up with a single mom and sometimes there were things we just didn't do because we couldn't. But there were plenty of things that we did do that made a lasting impression and I'm sure there are going to be times when Maya's going to remember them and want to share them."

Dean gave a low, mirthless laugh. "I hate to say it, but I don't think my sister did a whole lot with Maya. At first, she was so distraught over losing her husband that she was barely holding on by a thread. My parents stayed with her and I went and stayed with her. Maya was just a baby. Then she seemed to be doing better and we all sort of relaxed and went back to our own lives. We saw each other for holidays and whatnot, but I didn't realize just how bad things were until I showed up the morning that Karen died. There were things that Maya said and it didn't take long for me to realize that she was fairly self-sufficient."

Dammit. He really hadn't meant to get into all of this. Not when he finally had Abby alone.

She was still holding his hand, caressing it with her other. "You learn to be that way. Not only because a parent is neglectful – because mine wasn't – but you do it because you want to be helpful. It makes you feel like you're helping. My mom was always so tired from working two jobs that I wanted to learn to do stuff so I could help her."

"I wish I could say it was the same for Maya, but it wasn't. Unfortunately, she spent more time with the sitter than she spent with Karen. It kills me. I swear, every time I think I'm okay with it or that I'm used to it, Maya will say something that just breaks my heart all over again." He looked up at her sadly. "I hate that I wasn't there more or that I didn't know just how bad it all was for her."

"But you're here now," Abby reminded him. "And you're working so hard to make a good life for her. I can see such a difference in Maya. She's chatty and friendly and…I'll admit that she doesn't talk a whole lot about her mom, but she talks about you and all of the things the two of you are going to do together. What you're doing for her – *with* her – means a lot. You're doing a great job."

He wished he could believe her. Shaking his head, the only thing Dean knew was that this was not the conversation he wanted to have, so he did his best to change the subject.

"I'm really glad that you're here, Abby. And not just because of Maya, but…for me too. I can't believe that it took me so long to get to know you."

She laughed softly. "Well…I have a confession to make."

He looked at her expectantly.

"I used to wish that you'd want to get to know me. When you would come into the diner for breakfast, I always made sure I sat you in my section in hopes that you would talk to me and then I used to wish that you'd ask me out." She was blushing, looking at their hands as she confessed.

"Are you... you mean you were interested in me?" he asked, unable to believe that he had been that clueless.

She nodded and then looked up at him. "I was. I...I am." Pausing, she shook her head. "That's not the reason I offered to help with Maya. I want you to know that. One has nothing to do with the other. But...I don't want this to be weird for you."

"How could it possibly be weird? What are you talking about?"

"I just...I don't want you wondering why I'm here or what's prompting me to be here with you and Maya. I think she's a great kid and honestly, I see a lot of myself in her. I love her enthusiasm for dancing and I want to help her learn more about it and really see if it's something she wants to continue with."

"Abby, I'll admit that I had no idea that you...well, that you had feelings for me, but I know you're not the kind of person who would use a child to get close to anyone. To me," he said, his voice a little low, gruff. Taking his hand from hers, he reached up and caressed her cheek. "I'm just trying to figure out how we make this work. My life is...crazy right now. My time isn't my own and I have no idea when that's going to change – or if it ever will."

"And I totally get that," she replied. "I would never ask you to put time with me before your time with Maya. I guess…I guess we just sort of have to wait and see how it goes."

He frowned. "That's it? No plan? No…demand on when we'll be able to go out alone?"

She chuckled softly. "Dean, that's something you're going to learn about me. I don't really make plans too far ahead and I don't put demands on anyone. I'm fairly laid back and go with the flow even when it's probably not the best thing for me."

"That doesn't sound good."

"It's not. Not really." Abby paused and seemed to be considering her next words. "I'm the kind of person who will go out of my way for someone in need and not expect anything in return. I just do it because I want to. Sometimes people appreciate the help, other times they don't and ultimately I get taken advantage of. I try not to let that happen too much but sometimes it can't be helped."

"I certainly don't want to take advantage of you where Maya is concerned. I really do appreciate all that you're doing for her, for us. And if it gets to the point where you're feeling put upon, promise me you'll say something." He paused and shook his head, then let out a small laugh. "I tend to be a little more clueless, probably because I don't hang out with a lot of people. My job is fairly solitary and I've lived on my own for so many years. I'm figuring all of it out a little bit each day and I have to admit, this is a big transition for me."

"You mean with Maya?"

He nodded. "And with you." He shrugged. "You work at the gossip capital of Silver Dell Falls. I'm sure by now you know that everyone refers to me as a recluse."

She chuckled. "Sorry. But…okay. Yes. I do know that and it always bothered me when they said it."

"Why?"

Now it was her turn to shrug. "I don't know. It just seemed…wrong. Sad, actually. I hated to think of you being alone and cut off from the community."

"Well, I'm sure you also heard about what my family was like when I was growing up. Or more specifically, my sister."

Abby nodded. "I have. But…the first time I heard about it was right after she died. Before that…I don't know. It just never came up."

When Dean started discussing his family, he felt some tension start to ease from his shoulders. "So…I guess we're just going to take this day by day."

"I guess so," she agreed, a small smile playing at her lips.

They were silent for a few minutes and Dean took the time to look at her – to linger without an audience or without being rushed. "This is nice," he said softly, reaching up and caressing her cheek again.

"I have to agree."

"Did I thank you for baking the cookies?" he asked, inching just a little bit closer to her.

"You did," she answered just as softly. "Did I thank you for making dinner?"

"You did." He couldn't help but smile.

"Hmm…I guess there's nothing else for us to really talk about," she said with a dramatic sigh.

"Good," Dean said. "Because I'm really done with talking." Then he closed the distance between them, gently pulling her forward and claiming her lips with his.

The first time they'd kissed, it had been an impulse and slightly frantic before Maya had interrupted them. But now there were no interruptions, no one watching, and rather than go for fast and frantic, Dean wanted to savor. Explore. Taste and tease. Abby melted against him and as his arms wrapped around her, he did what he'd been dying to do for what seemed like weeks.

He reached up, pulled the band from her hair and ran his hand through it.

So soft – like silk – and it felt really good against his skin. Fisting it in his hand, he pulled her closer and Abby went willingly. Her own hands were raking up into his hair and he had no idea who moved first, but soon they were lying down on the sofa. He was on his back and Abby was sprawled out on top of him – every inch of her pressed up against him.

She weighed next to nothing and when he let his one free hand roam up and down her back, down over the curve of her slender waist and then lower to cup her bottom, he couldn't help but imagine how soft her skin would feel. Or how those long, sleek limbs would feel wrapped around him.

His mouth skimmed her jaw, her throat sighed his name and that's when he knew they had to stop. It had been too long since he'd been with a woman and Maya was just down the hall and…

Abby lifted up slightly as if reading his mind, her breathing ragged. "Wow."

Dean caressed her cheek and jaw and sighed. "If we were alone in the house right now…"

She nodded. "I know. That's what I was thinking too."

"But we're not and…" He paused and shifted them so they were sitting up a little straighter. "I want you, Abby. I knew once we were alone that I'd want to kiss you and I thought that would be enough, but once I did…"

"It was pretty intense."

"I wanted to go slow. I'm sorry. I should have had a little more control."

Abby chuckled and reached out, taking one of his hands in hers. "I don't think either of us had much control for a few minutes there and really, it was just kissing."

"Just kissing?" he teased.

"You know what I mean," she said shyly.

Nodding, he squeezed her hand. "I know. I don't think I've had such an exciting make-out session since I was about seventeen."

They shifted again until they were side by side with Abby's head on his shoulder. "Maybe we could watch a little TV or something."

"Sounds like a plan." Dean reached for the remote and they channel surfed for a few minutes before he decided to turn on Netflix so they'd have more options. "Do we want to laugh, think, or have the bejesus scared out of us?" Abby laughed out loud and Dean really loved the sound. "What's your show of choice? Binge watch anything lately?"

"You know, I haven't. When I'm home and have free time, I tend to dance and work on choreography for the classes."

"Really? Even after teaching all afternoon you still want to go home and dance? I would think you'd be exhausted and want to get off your feet."

She shrugged. "It invigorates me. But there are definitely days when all I want to do is crash on the couch with about ten pounds of junk food and just zone out for a while. I don't do it, but the thought is there."

"Okay, so what should we binge on?" he asked softly. "And do I need to get out some junk food?"

"I wouldn't say no to a couple more cookies…"

Dean carefully moved and stood up. "You scroll around and see if you find something of interest and I'll get us some cookies and…"

"Milk. The word you're looking for is milk," she teased. "There is no other beverage to drink with them."

Laughing, Dean made his way to the kitchen. Five minutes later, he was back beside her on the sofa and saw that she had chosen *Orange is the New Black*.

"I don't think I've watched this," he said, reaching for a cookie.

"Me either. But I hear people talking about it all the time. I guess I'd like to see what all the fuss is about. Is that okay?"

"Absolutely."

And with Abby curled up beside him, they shared a plate of cookies and he finally learned the appeal of the whole "Netflix and chill" craze.

# FIVE

For every one thing that had gone right for the following week, something else went wrong. Well, that wasn't completely accurate. It was just the one thing.

Not enough time alone with Abby.

And Dean was slowly losing his mind.

They saw each other every day – they'd even had dinner together twice – but Maya had been with them. Whenever they spent time together was great – they would laugh and have fun and he found himself relaxing more and more and settling into his newfound role of single parent. He was even enjoying it. But right now, he couldn't help but focus on how different things would be if he didn't have to be a responsible single parent.

He could take Abby out on a proper date.

She could spend the night with him at his place.

Or he could spend the night with her at her place.

It wasn't particularly helpful for him to keep harping on it and yet…it was never far from his mind. When he was alone in his car on the way to and from work? He thought about it. When he was out walking a piece of property for work? He thought about it. And when he would show up at the dance studio and see Abby moving around in nothing but one of her leotards, tights and those little wrap skirts? Hell yeah he thought about it.

Now here he was on a Friday afternoon trying to figure out a way to find some time alone with her. They were already planning another Netflix night at his house the following night but…damn. It felt wrong that he wasn't taking her out someplace.

How ironic that he'd spent a large portion of his life trying to stay inside and away from any kind of social activity and now that he was more than ready to go out, he was forced to stay in.

Unbelievable.

Thanksgiving was just a little less than a week away. Being that his parents had just traveled for his sister's funeral, they already let him know that they wouldn't be making the trip for Thanksgiving this year. And he'd had no problem letting them know that he wasn't prepared to travel again either. Maybe that was the wrong attitude to have – after all, they all normally spent the holiday together.

At Karen's.

At first, Dean wasn't sure of what he wanted to do or how he was going to handle it, but when he talked to Abby about it, she told him that she was going to be alone this year too. Her mom wasn't coming in for Thanksgiving because she was going to come and spend Christmas with her. Their plans just seemed to fall into place from there that they'd spend the day together. Abby was going to come over and they were all going to work together to make a Thanksgiving feast.

Maya was beyond thrilled with the idea. She'd been talking for days about helping stuff the turkey and how she was going to learn to mash real potatoes. Overall, their Thanksgiving was shaping up to be a good day for all of them.

If he could just get over the disappointment in their lack of privacy and alone time.

Walking into the community center, he waved to Kathy Jones and was just going to keep walking when she called out to him again. Turning around, he walked over to the desk. "Hey, Kathy. What's up?"

"Well, I was kind of hoping I could ask a favor," she said a bit hesitantly.

"A favor?" It really did seem kind of odd. He'd known Kathy since high school but they had never really had a reason to talk since then. He knew she was married and had a couple of kids and obviously she worked for the town, but other than that, he couldn't imagine him being able to help her with anything.

"My youngest daughter Jenny is in Abby's class with your niece Maya. They're also in the same class at school," she began.

"Oh," he said, still not sure where she was going with all of this.

"Anyway, Jenny's birthday is tomorrow and she's having a party – a slumber party – and…well…I know it's short notice but she would love for Maya to come! I know this is all kind of new to you, and maybe Maya's not ready for a sleepover, but…I wanted to ask you first before Jenny said anything. And believe me, she's been dying to say something."

If he could, he'd jump over the desk and kiss Kathy. He knew he had to play it cool. It would seem odd if he were overly anxious about sending his niece off to a sleepover with a group of people who didn't really know. He wracked his brain for the appropriate questions.

"So…what time would she need to be there tomorrow?"

Kathy's entire face lit up with joy. "Oh, you're really okay with letting her come over?"

"Well…"

"It's going to be wonderful. Sam and I are both going to be home along with our two older daughters, Michele and Amy, who will be helping out with the younger girls. We've had six girls say yes and then you add Jenny and – hopefully – Maya, and that will be eight little girls." She fanned herself for dramatic effect.

"That sounds a bit overwhelming," he commented, mainly because just the thought of it scared the hell out of him. He was thankful Maya hadn't asked to have a sleepover at their house.

Yet.

"We're asking all of the parents to bring the girls over around three tomorrow afternoon. We're going to play games and watch a movie and we're going to order pizza for dinner and it's just going to be a ton of fun!"

Dean had no idea why she would think that. It sounded like torture to him. "Um…what time would I need to pick her up on Sunday?"

"Some of the girls are getting picked up early – like around ten – because they're going to church with their families, but the majority are staying until after lunch. So really, it's completely up to you as to when you'd like to get her."

His heart was beating wildly in his chest as his mind raced with all of the new opportunities the weekend held. He could take Abby out on a date. They could have some time alone.

One of them could spend the night – like an adult sleepover.

It was almost too good to let himself imagine.

"Are you sure you're okay with letting her come to the party? I wasn't sure if she was struggling with separation anxiety or…you know…anything like that," Kathy said quietly.

"I honestly don't know. This will be the first time that we're going to try this."

Reaching across the desk, she patted his hand. "Tell you what, why don't you talk to her first? I know she's in there with Abby. It's so wonderful how she's taken Maya under her wing. The two of them just look so precious together!"

He had to agree.

"So talk to her – maybe get Abby's input too – and let me know before you leave. And if she's not ready to do it, then that's okay too," Kathy said. "We can always try again at another time."

"Sounds good. Thanks, Kathy." Dean waved and turned to walk into the classroom. Abby was finishing up and giving her students some extra instructions since there wouldn't be any classes next week due to the holiday. He took a seat and waited for her to finish. Once the class was dismissed, he made his way across the room toward Maya who was doing her homework quietly in the corner.

"Hey, kiddo," he said, crouching down beside her. "What are you working on?"

She shrugged but didn't look at him.

Odd. She was normally chatty when he came to pick her up – anxious to tell him about her day and everything that happened at school. He looked at the picture she was coloring. "This is a great picture," he praised. "Can we hang it on the refrigerator when we get home?"

Another shrug.

Out of the corner of his eye, he noticed Abby motioning to him. Kissing Maya on the head, he rose and walked across the room. "What's going on? Has she been like this all afternoon?"

Abby nodded. "She was upset when she got off the bus because she heard some of the girls in her class talking about a slumber party and she didn't get invited. My heart just about broke in two for her. I offered to let her come and have a sleepover at my place, but that didn't work." She sighed. "I just didn't even know what to say to her."

"You may not believe this, but I was just talking to Kathy out at the front desk about this exact thing."

"A slumber party?"

He nodded. "It's her daughter who's having the party. She said Jenny takes ballet at the same time as Maya."

Abby's eyes went wide. "Maya didn't tell me who it was. She didn't mention any names. Oh, no wonder she was so upset. The two of them have really become buddies." She turned and looked at Maya sitting in the corner looking sad. Turning back to Dean she said, "Please tell me she was inviting Maya to that party!"

He nodded. "She wanted to run it by me before Jenny said anything to Maya. She was afraid that maybe Maya was dealing with some separation anxiety and might not be ready to venture out to a sleepover yet."

"Do you think she is?"

Dean shrugged. "Honestly, I don't know. She mentioned a couple of weeks ago about hoping that someday she'd get to sleep at a friend's house, but she also talked about how often her mom would dump her off at the babysitter's house to sleep there. So really, it's anyone's guess how she's going to handle this."

Abby considered him for a minute. "Why don't we go and talk to her?" Then she stopped and shook her head. "Sorry. Totally not my place. You go and talk to her and I'll get this room cleaned up so we can go."

She turned to walk away but Dean grabbed her hand and pulled her back. "I kind of liked your first suggestion," he said quietly. "I'm not always good with stuff like this. It would be great if you could sit with us and sort of…smooth things over if I screw it up."

"Are you sure?"

He nodded. "Please."

And together they walked over and sat down with Maya. She gave them each a quick glance before going back to her coloring. Dean looked at Abby for some sort of help on whether she wanted to speak or if he should go first.

"You got a lot done on that," Abby said and Dean was happy that she took the lead.

Maya shrugged.

"So listen, I know you said that you didn't want to have a sleep over at my house but I think your uncle has something far more exciting that you might be interested in."

Maya looked up at Dean with mild curiosity. "What?"

Dean smiled broadly – he knew the key was in the delivery. "When I got here a little while ago, I stopped and said hello to Kathy Jones. She's Jenny's mom."

Clearly that was the wrong thing to say because Maya began to furiously color again.

"She said there's a slumber party tomorrow night but she wasn't sure if you wanted to go," Dean said quickly.

That got his niece's attention. She looked up at him. "Why did she think that?"

"Well," he started carefully, "she knows that you're new to the town and the school and she thought that maybe you weren't ready to go to a slumber party yet. She asked me about it."

"Did you tell her that I always wanted to go to a slumber party?" Maya asked, jumping to her feet.

Dean couldn't help but smile at the instant change in her demeanor. "Of course I did!"

Quite possibly for the first time ever, she seemed uncertain of what she was supposed to do. "So…" She looked at Dean and then Abby and then back to Dean. "Does this mean I can go? I'm invited to the slumber party?"

Dean nodded. "It sure does!"

"Yeah!" She flung herself into his arms and hugged him tight. His own arms banded around her. After a minute, she squirmed out of them. "I don't have a sleeping bag! Or…or…a suitcase to bring with me! We have to go and get a present and…and…Jenny really likes dolls just like me, so can we get her a doll? Or maybe something else?" She turned to Abby. "What do you think we should get her? Will you go to the store with us and help me pick something and then help me wrap it really pretty for Jenny?"

Abby laughed and said, "Of course I will. Why don't we go ask Jenny's mom what she thinks Jenny would like?"

"Okay!" Without waiting, Maya ran from the room and Dean could already hear her calling out "I get to go to the slumber party!"

Waiting until he knew Maya was out of the room, Dean turned and moved in close to Abby. "So…"

She grinned and placed a hand on his chest. "So…"

"I was thinking that maybe you and I could go out tomorrow. We could go to dinner and just eat a grown-up meal and have grown-up conversation. What do you think?"

Her smile grew. "I think I like that idea a lot." She paused. "Are you okay with this?"

Dean looked at her oddly. "With what? Having dinner out? Absolutely. I know everyone in town thinks I'm reclusive but…"

She chuckled and stopped him. "No, no, no…sorry. That wasn't what I meant. I meant to ask if you are okay with Maya sleeping out. This is kind of a big deal."

"Is it?" Seriously, was it?

"Well, maybe more for her than for you but still. I know she's excited and it all sounds great…"

"But…"

"But," she continued, "a first sleepover can be scary and you need to be prepared that she might get homesick and want to come home."

Dean shook his head. "Not gonna happen."

"How can you be so sure?"

"When she lived back in Pennsylvania, she used to sleep at the babysitter's house, so I know she's okay with sleeping out. And this is something she's been talking about – like some sort of big dream of hers – so I think she's going to be fine."

Abby looked at him skeptically. "If you say so."

"Are you trying to get out of going out on a date with me?" he teased, his voice low and gruff.

She closed the distance between them. "Not a chance. If anything, I was thinking about us having a grown-up sleepover – you know, to go along with that grown-up dinner and conversation you were talking about."

He laughed out loud and gave her a quick kiss before taking a step back. "I better get out there and talk with Kathy and get all the details confirmed. Want to come to the mall to get all of the supplies with us?"

"I wouldn't miss it."

As Dean walked out of the classroom and toward the information desk, he had a little pep in his step and realized he had a lot to look forward to.

His niece was making friends and settling in better than he'd expected.

Thanksgiving was going to be spent making some new traditions with Abby and Maya.

Saturday afternoon couldn't get here quickly enough.

****

"Pink sleeping bag?"

"Check."

"Princess pillow?"

"Check."

"Superbly wrapped holiday ballerina doll?"

Maya giggled and held up the wrapped present. "Check!"

"Pink deluxe suitcase filled with princess pajamas, slippers, clean clothes, underwear, toothbrush, toothpaste, hair brush and…favorite stuffed bear?"

Maya skipped across the room and stood next to her brand new suitcase. "Check, check, check, check…" She stopped and sighed. "Ugh…like a million checks! Can we go now? Please?"

Abby stood up and surveyed the pile of things they'd just gone over. "I sure hope we have enough room in the car for all this stuff," she said dramatically. "I would hate to have to take two cars over to Jenny's or to have to leave you here."

"Abby," Maya giggled. "Uncle Dean has lots of room in his car! We fit a whole bunch of stuff in it when I had to move here!"

"I think there was a trailer too…" Abby teased.

That just made Maya laugh harder. "That was for the big stuff. This isn't big!"

"But there is a lot of it," Abby commented.

Dean walked into the room and looked at the two of them and then at the pile of stuff. "You all ready to go?"

Maya nodded furiously. "Yes! Yes! Yes!"

Walking across the room, Abby smiled at him. "I think someone's a little excited about the slumber party."

"She's not the only one," he murmured.

*Oh my…*

Who was she kidding? Abby knew she was definitely looking forward to their night out too. They'd talked about it and decided that they'd take Maya to Jenny's together and then they were going to go do the Thanksgiving shopping – her idea – and bring it back to her house before heading to the city for dinner. And then…

"Come on, you guys!" Maya yelled from the front door. "It's time! We gotta go! I don't want the slumber party to start without me!"

Abby scooped up the gift and the pillow while Dean grabbed Maya's suitcase and sleeping bag. They walked out to the living room to see Maya bouncing on her toes. "Let's go!" Dean said.

The chatter was non-stop the whole drive over and even though it seemed like Dean was having a hard time keeping up, Abby couldn't help but feel pleased – happy, really – that he and Maya were making such great strides in their relationship. She thought back to that first day and could easily picture the stress on his face, his rigid posture and the uncertainty in everything he said just as easily as she remembered a less boisterous version of Maya. Look at them now!

Jenny only lived a couple of blocks away from Dean, so the drive over was blessedly short. Maya ran from the car as soon as she was out of her booster seat and made her way to the front door. Jenny was equally anxious because she was already waiting there with the door open.

Within minutes they had Maya's belongings inside and were talking to Kathy about the plans for the night and they all exchanged phone numbers in case of an emergency. Dean made Kathy promise to call or text if Maya seemed even remotely uncomfortable about staying over and even though she agreed, she told him she couldn't imagine that happening.

More of the girls started to arrive and Abby gave Maya a quick kiss on the cheek and wished her a fun night before stepping back and letting Dean kiss her goodbye too. It wasn't until they were heading back to the truck that she noticed he looked...pensive.

"Are you okay?" she asked.

He shrugged as they climbed back into the car. "I know she's excited and that it's going to be a lot of fun but...I don't know. When I said goodbye to her, suddenly she looked so small. Obviously she's not too young for this because all of the girls here are the same age but it just felt weird. I didn't...I never thought I'd feel like this."

Abby reached over and squeezed his hand, unsure of what she could possibly say to that. She had no idea what he must be feeling. It was one thing to love a relative, but now Maya was more than a niece to him. He was a father figure – a father, period –  and from what Dean just shared, it would seem that the transition of those feelings had already begun.

What an amazing thing to be able to witness, she thought to herself and smiled.

They drove across town in silence and when he pulled into the grocery store parking lot, she had to admit that this seemed a little odd. Dean parked and then sat there for a moment. Abby turned in her seat and faced him.

"Let's not do this."

Dean's head whipped around toward her. "What?"

She waved toward the store. "The food shopping. Let's not do it today. I can totally do it on my own tomorrow. Let's go and find something else to do."

"But…I was kind of looking forward to this."

"Seriously?" she deadpanned. "It's grocery shopping. Nothing exciting about it."

Her hand was still holding his and he twisted them around slightly until their fingers were twined together. "It's not about the food," he said with a hint of shyness. "It's just about spending time with you." His gaze met hers. "I can't even begin to describe it but…I just really enjoy being with you. Spending time with you. For the first time in I don't even know how long, I'm actually looking forward to Thanksgiving. And…you know…Christmas."

Her heart squeezed happily in her chest. He was thinking ahead – about the holidays and her.

What more could she possibly ask for?

With a hopeful look on his face, Abby knew she should just go with it and get the shopping out of the way. It was probably going to be fun. With an exaggerated sigh, she grabbed her purse. "Okay. Let's do this."

If it were possible, she'd say that he reminded her of Maya as he got out of the car. He was clearly excited about this and happy and…completely and utterly adorable. He met her on the passenger side of the car and gave her a loud, smacking kiss on the lips.

"This is gonna be great!" he said enthusiastically. "We're going to make some great food and desserts! Can we bake a pie? Do you know how to bake pies? I've never done that before but I always thought a homemade apple pie was the best dessert after the Thanksgiving dinner!"

Yup. She could totally see the family resemblance now.

And while walking up and down the aisles of the store, she saw it even more. He had her laughing almost the entire time and Abby found herself telling him to put stuff back on the shelves because they didn't need it for their meal. And like a typical kid, he would pout when she vetoed one of his choices.

And she didn't care how much he protested, they did not need to bake a chocolate lava cake or a cookies and cream pie or peanut butter marshmallow cookies on top of the apple pie for them to have for dessert. There was only the three of them!

"You're a spoilsport," Dean murmured as he made his way down the frozen food aisle. "Can we at least get ice cream to go with the apple pie?"

She rolled her eyes. "Look, if you want to make all of those desserts and bring them with you on Thanksgiving Day, then that's fine. But I'm not going to have time to make them – and I still think it's overkill. Maya will be bouncing off the walls and I have a feeling you will be too."

He chuckled. "You may be right. I guess I never gave much thought to the meal before." He shrugged. "We all always met at Karen's because she had Maya and it was harder for her to travel. My parents were always there and my mom did the cooking. It was a traditional meal, never changed. I just thought it could be fun to change things up a bit."

It didn't take a genius to figure out what he was doing. Dean was trying to guilt her a little bit so he could get his way.

"You'd think for someone whose been reading all these parenting books and websites that you'd recognize this pattern of behavior," she said lightly, grabbing a container of strawberry ice cream from the freezer case.

"What do you mean?" he asked innocently.

"Oh, please. The whole guilt trip thing. You've mentioned – more than once, might I add – that Maya's tried using it on you to get her way and here you are trying to use it on me!" Unable to help herself, she burst out laughing.

He didn't even try to look innocent. "What can I say? I know I tend to cave when Maya does it so I thought I'd give it a try."

Playfully, Abby punched him in the arm. "Baby steps," she said. "We're making enough food for a small army. We'll re-think the desserts for Christmas. Deal?"

"Deal."

Yeah. She really liked that he was thinking ahead.

# Six

It had been the perfect day.

And a perfect date.

Now as they were driving back through Silver Bell Falls, Dean suddenly wasn't so sure about the rest of the night. He knew what he wanted – had been fantasizing about it ever since...well...for a while now – but now that it was here, he wasn't so sure. After all, this was technically their first date. With a silent sigh, he turned onto her street – resigned to be satisfied with kissing her goodnight at the door and heading home alone.

They were both quiet as he pulled into the driveway and turned off the car. For a moment, he simply sat there – willing himself not to be disappointed.

Or at least not to let that disappointment show.

Easier said than done.

Climbing from the car, he walked around to the passenger side as Abby was getting out. The air was cool and when she smiled at him and let out a small breath, it was visible. He took her by the hand and led her to the front door, unwilling to keep her out in the cold any longer than was necessary.

"I had a great time today," Abby said softly, unlocking the door. She stepped inside and motioned for Dean to follow.

"I did too," he replied, but didn't move.

She tilted her head as she studied him. "Aren't you coming in?"

*God yes*, was what he really wanted to say. More than anything. "It's late," he said instead and it even sounded lame to his own ears.

Abby looked over her shoulder and then back at Dean. "It's nine-thirty."

Yeah. Lame. He was about to explain himself when Abby spoke up again.

"Well...I guess it has been a long day. I'm sure Maya gets up early and all that." She sighed softly. "I really did have a great time today, Dean. I can't remember the last time I just went out and had a dinner that wasn't at the diner or some sort of fast food so...thank you."

Her smile was soft and sweet and...damn. Why was this so hard? Why was he making such a big deal out of it? They had talked about it and at the time she'd been on board but...

"What time do you have to pick her up tomorrow?" Abby asked, once again interrupting his inner dialogue.

"Um...after lunch. Kathy said some of the girls were leaving early but she said Maya could stay until after lunch."

Nodding, Abby smiled and just...looked at him.

"I'm sure you'll enjoy having your house to yourself and to have some peace and quiet. I know that had to be a hard adjustment for you to make."

He nodded.

*This is ridiculous*, he mentally chided himself. All of the heat was coming out of her house because he was being an idiot and refusing to go inside. Just because he accepted her invitation to go in didn't mean he had to stay the night. He could just go in and maybe hang out for a bit. Watch a little TV. Or maybe…

"Dean?"

"Hmm?"

Before he could even blink, Abby reached out, pulled him by his wool scarf into the house and shut the door. The house was dark and – thanks to him – a little cool, but he was able to see the look of amusement on Abby's face as she moved in close. One of her delicate hands rested on his chest while the other raked up into his hair.

He really liked when she did that.

"Let me ask you something," she began quietly – her voice going slightly sultry. "Do you want to go home?"

Unable to speak, he simply shook his head.

"Okay." She gave him a curt nod before moving in even closer. They were practically touching from head to toe. Those big green eyes looked up at him and he knew he'd been fighting with himself over nothing.

"I kind of felt like I was being presumptuous," he admitted. "We had a great day together and...well...this was our first real date. I didn't want you to feel like I was pressuring you or pushing you into something you didn't want."

"We'd already talked about it," she said simply. "Hell, I almost skipped dessert because I was really looking forward to coming back here and finally being alone with you."

His own dark eyes went wide. "Really?"

Abby nodded. "Honestly, I would have been fine with grabbing a pizza and staying in."

Dean couldn't help the laugh that came out. "Sure, now you tell me!" he teased right before he reached up and cupped Abby's cheek in one hand. He stroked the soft skin and then he turned serious. "I meant what I said, Abby. I just didn't want you to think that this was all I wanted. I really enjoyed going out with you today and I think you know enough about me to know that it's not something I usually do."

"I know. That's why I didn't throw out my pizza suggestion," she said, her own expression serious. "It means a lot to me that you were willing to go out tonight and leave your comfort zone. You didn't have to." Then she got up on her toes and placed a soft kiss on the side of his throat. "But I'm really glad you did."

There were so many things swirling around in his head that he wanted to say, but none of it seemed...enough. He wasn't good with talking about his feelings. That wasn't his style, but he could show her.

He could spend all night showing her.

Leaning down, he kissed her. It was the kind of kiss that you eased into, that built up momentum and left you anxious for the next one. And he sure was anxious for the next one. And the one after that. Abby let out a soft hum that he actually could feel and knew she felt exactly as he did.

It was all the encouragement he needed.

Sighing her name as his lips reluctantly left hers to travel across the soft skin of her cheek and down the slender column of her throat, he let his hands begin to wander. For weeks, he'd admired her lithe body, wondered what it would feel like under his hands. Together they worked to take her coat and scarf off before doing the same with his.

They didn't bother with propriety – like hanging the garments up – they simply let them drop to the floor. Abby initiated the next kiss as she slowly led him to her bedroom, walking backwards through the darkened house. Once inside her room, she broke the kiss and smiled up at him.

A quick glance around showed him a room with one small lamp lit and a bed that was partially turned down –

as if in anticipation. He looked at Abby with a sheepish grin. "Had I known…"

"This is perfect," she said softly. "Although...now I feel like I'm the one who was being presumptuous."

Dean shook his head. "Never. I think this just shows that we're both feeling the same way." He paused and caressed her cheek. "And I'm hoping we're both going to be feeling a lot better."

Abby's smile was slow and shy and even in the dim light he saw her blush again – could almost feel the heat creep into her cheeks. Without a word, she took a step back and slipped her shoes off – her eyes never leaving his. Tonight she'd worn her long hair loose and in this lighting it looked soft and glossy with a hint of blue to it. It fascinated him.

Before he could comment on it, Abby pulled her sweater up and over her head and then all rational thought left him.

Her body was so slim, so...everything. His hands began to twitch with the need to touch her. Wearing deep purple lace to cover her breasts, she looked so damn perfect.

Then she sighed his name.

And he was lost.

#### \*\*\*\*

It was late.

Much later than Abby normally stayed awake.

But there was a very good reason for it.

Dean was wrapped around her and it felt absolutely glorious. In all of her fantasies about him – and there had been many in the last year – never had it been like this. She had a feeling he'd be incredibly gentle with her – because of his normal quiet disposition – but she never expected the wildness in him.

And she loved it.

Like seriously loved it.

With the slightest bit of encouragement from her, he'd gone from careful and cautious with her – as if he was afraid she'd break – to a slightly dominant, demanding and thorough lover.

"You're quiet," he whispered and even the sound of his low voice was enough to make her tingle.

"I'm simply enjoying being here like this with you."

"Are you sure? I got a little...carried away."

Abby heard the hesitancy in his voice and had a feeling he'd be worried about it. "I believe I thoroughly encouraged the carrying and believe me when I say I enjoyed it." Turning in his arms, she faced him and smiled. "And...I do believe I wouldn't mind having you get carried away again."

Dean chuckled softly. "I'm not sure what I'm supposed to say to that."

She laughed with him. "How about exactly what you're thinking?"

"I would but 'yippee' just seems a little unmanly."

They both laughed as Dean hugged her close and kissed her on the top of her head. "Abby," he sighed.

"Hmm?"

"I have a confession to make."

"Okay," she said quietly.

"I love watching you dance," he said.

Well...that wasn't what she was expecting. At all. "Really?"

He nodded. "I'm actually a little in awe of the way you dance and move and..." He stopped.

Abby sat up a little and looked at him. "What? What were you going to say?"

"Never mind," he said shyly and tried to pull her in for another kiss.

But her curiosity got the better of her. "Uh-uh. Come on. What were you going to say?"

Dean sighed. Loudly. Rolling onto his back, he flung an arm over his eyes as if he were embarrassed to look at her. "I kind of...dammit." Another sigh. "I kind of fantasized about watching you dance. Just for me."

Wow. That was totally unexpected too. "Like...a striptease?" she asked, slightly confused.

He shook his head. "No. More like...just doing what you do in class. But...just for me. And maybe...just wearing something sexy."

Ah...now she got it. "Like maybe just my underwear or a tutu?"

He groaned. "I'm horrible. You're probably thinking I'm a total perv right now, right?"

She couldn't help but laugh. "No! I just...I never had anybody say something like that to me."

"Please don't hate me or think I'm weird." He cursed. "I'm an idiot. Just...forget I said anything, all right?"

It would be easy to tell him yes and move on but...the idea sort of intrigued her. Moving from the bed, she moved in the darkness and pulled her lingerie back on.

"Abby..."

She ignored him as she made her way around the room. She found her iPod and plugged it into her portable speakers. Next, she twisted her hair up and...

"Don't," he said, his voice low and gruff.

"Don't what?"

"Leave it down. Please. If you can."

For a moment, she stood frozen and uncertain. He'd really put some thought into this. He was about to say something but she cut him off. "Shh...it's fine. Really." Turning, Abby chose a selection from her iPod – a classical piece that she usually used when she was dancing around the house as part of her morning routine. When she turned around, Dean was sitting a little more upright with the pillows stacked behind him so he could watch her.

Her bedroom wasn't overly spacious, but it offered enough room for her to do several moves to showcase what she sometimes did in class. The ballet classes were really for beginners and whenever she did dance alone, it was normally to teach the steps to the class. Only occasionally did she really dance just to stretch out and really show the class what she could do. Sometimes it was done at the request of the girls because they enjoyed watching her dance – and Abby really enjoyed doing it for them.

Sort of like how she was enjoying this now.

Maybe not the lingerie part – she was a little self-conscious about that, about her body in general – but judging by the way Dean was watching her right now, he didn't feel the same way about her body as she did.

Thank God.

Normally that wasn't an issue for her – sort of. No man had ever complained about her body. But this was the first time she was doing something that was so blatantly showcasing it.

And that was saying something.

Sex was intimate. The act of making love meant baring your body to your partner, but the fact that Dean wanted to see her dance with next to nothing on felt intimate on a whole other level.

The music started and Abby took a steadying breath, forcing all thoughts of Dean, her body – and her underwear – out of her mind and letting the music speak to her. She moved. Her body flowed and spun and paused and simply let itself be led by the music. It wasn't easy in the limited space, but Abby found herself moving instinctively – doing moves that she normally only used when she was alone. And minutes later – when the music stopped – she simply held the pose.

And her breath.

She never saw or heard Dean move and yet suddenly he was in front of her. Relaxing her pose, she looked up at him and the look in his eyes showed a myriad of emotions. It was heady and exciting and a little bit terrifying.

"What did you…?"

She never got to finish. Dean's lips claimed hers in a kiss that was so fierce, so carnal that she simply melted against him. He lifted her as she wrapped her legs around his waist and let him carry her back to the bed. She couldn't breathe, couldn't think and still he kissed her. He peeled the silk and lace from her body and as he moved against her a second time, Abby had to wonder how she had lived this long without ever feeling like this.

\*\*\*\*

In the morning, Dean simply enjoyed the act of holding Abby while she slept.

At least, that was his plan for a little while. Eventually he'd wake her and make love to her again before he had to leave. And damn, he so did not want to leave.

Last night was...there were no words. Making love to Abby for the first time was incredible. Watching her dance? Well, that was the most sensual and erotic thing he'd ever seen and holy hell, the image was going to be burned into his brain permanently. Watching Abby dance, in general, was one thing, but watching her dance just for him? There were no words.

Turning slightly, he looked over at the clock and saw that it was after nine. They had several hours but...maybe he was being selfish. Maybe Abby had things to do today and he should be attempting to get up and get out of her way. He was just about to move when he felt her kiss his shoulder and his chest. She was curled up against him with her hand resting low on his stomach and clearly, she was waking up.

A man could easily get used to this kind of an alarm clock.

"Mmm…" she purred against his skin. "Good morning."

It certainly was. "Good morning."

Abby stretched right before she slowly climbed on top of him, straddling him.

Yeah, a man could definitely get used to this.

"What time is it?" she asked sleepily, her eyes never leaving his.

"Just a little after nine."

A slow smile crept across her face. "Good. We have plenty of time. I was afraid I'd slept too long."

Dean didn't need to ask what she was talking about. Reaching out, he cupped her breasts before letting his hands roam up over her face and into that glorious mane of hair. His hands gently fisted there for a moment and he heard her soft hiss of breath. He murmured her name.

"I should be a good hostess and offer you breakfast, but…"

He shook his head. "This is much better than breakfast."

She laughed softly. "I don't know...I've been told I make spectacular pancakes."

For a moment, he pretended to consider her words. "Pancakes, huh? I guess this could wait." Instead of stopping, he moved under her, rubbing in all the right places.

The quiet moan that escaped her lips told Dean she was no more interested in breakfast right now than he was. He moved again. And again. And with each stroke Abby's breath hitched until she was practically panting. She chanted his name and began to move with him. Pulling her down, he kissed her. It was hot and wet and a little bit sloppy and yet it was perfect. And when they broke apart, she looked down at him and smiled.

Hell, they'd be lucky if they made it out of bed for lunch.

# Seven

"And then we had pizza! And I got to sit next to Jenny! We watched a movie and then had popcorn and cupcakes. I had a chocolate one with pink icing. There were vanilla ones too but I really like the chocolate ones the best!"

Maya had been in the car for all of five minutes and Dean wasn't sure she'd stopped to take a breath yet. He knew this sleepover had been a big deal to her and he was more than happy to let her chatter away about how much fun she had. It made him feel good to see her so excited.

"So can I? Can I Uncle Dean?"

Crap! What had he missed? "Um...sorry. What did you ask?" Looking in the rearview mirror, he saw his niece frown at him.

"I asked if I could sleep at Jenny's next weekend too!"

He wanted to say "hell yes" but figured they probably had to ask about that. "We'll talk to Jenny's mom on Monday. It's Thanksgiving week and I don't know if Jenny and her family will be in town. But if they are and her mom says it's okay, then I'm good with it too."

"Yeah!" she cried. "Thanks, Uncle Dean! You're the best!"

He wasn't so sure. As much as he could say he was doing it for her happiness, the truth was that he was also looking forward to having another night with Abby. For the foreseeable future, this was how it was going to be – stolen moments and grabbing a night alone when they could. It wasn't ideal and he wasn't thrilled about it, but it was their reality for now,

"Uncle Dean?"

Glancing at her in the mirror, he said, "Yes?"

"How come you're not married?"

"Um…"

"Did you have a wife and she died? Like my mom and dad?"

Oh hell… "Um…" Luckily, they were pulling into their driveway. Dean knew he wasn't going to be able to ignore her questions, but he certainly didn't want to have this talk in the car.

"Everyone at the party had a mom and a dad. You know, who were both alive and not in heaven. I told them that my mommy just died and that made me sad. Then Jenny's mom came over and hugged me and that's when we had the cupcakes. Then I wasn't so sad."

Dean climbed from the car and helped Maya get out. When they were inside, he asked her to sit down with him on the couch. She looked up at him – her big blue eyes as wide as saucers –  as she waited.

"You know that it's okay to be sad about your mom, right?" he began. When Maya nodded, he reached for her hand and held it in his. "And I want you to know that whenever you want to talk about that, about being sad or even if you just want to talk about your mom, you can come to me. She was my sister and...I miss her too."

Maya's face turned thoughtful, then serious. "You do?"

Dean nodded. "I really do. She was my big sister and I loved her." He squeezed her hand. "And it's okay to be sad, Maya. And sometimes it's going to be hard because...well...your friends won't be able to understand what you're feeling."

"Because their mommies are here and not in heaven," Maya said solemnly.

Dean nodded again. "Exactly. And I know it's going to be hard sometimes but I promise you that I'm always going to be here for you. It's not the same as your mom being here and I know that, but I just...I want you to know that I'll do whatever I can to make a good life for us."

She studied him for a long moment. "Are you going to get married?"

Damn. The kid didn't hold back on her questions, did she? He figured he owed her an honest answer. "I don't know. I always thought I'd get married someday, but...it's not something I'm thinking about right now. Right now I want to work on getting you and I settled into our life together. There's school and my job and the holidays are almost here and…"

"Did you get a turkey with Abby?" Maya interrupted.

"I sure did. It's over at Abby's house and she's going to make it for us."

Maya pulled her hand from his and jumped up so she was sitting on her knees on the sofa beside him – all traces of her sadness from moments ago, gone. "Do you think she'll let me help her with it? I know I didn't like to touch the chicken the last time I cooked with her, but I want to help with the turkey!"

Dealing with a five-year-old was beyond confusing. Maya's attention span was short and sometimes it was hard to keep up with her because she continually changed the subject. "You can ask her tomorrow after school. I'm sure she'd love for you to help her," he said and hoped he was right. For all he knew, Abby had her own tradition with preparing the Thanksgiving turkey that didn't involve having a curious kindergartener hovering over her shoulder.

"Okay," Maya said and then climbed off the couch. "Can I have a snack now?"

"Uh…sure." Rising, Dean went to the kitchen with Maya skipping behind him and helped her decide on some cookies and milk. He joined her at the kitchen table where they finished off the rest of the cookies they'd baked with Abby.

"I don't have school on Wednesday," Maya said around a mouthful of a chocolate chip cookie. "Or Thursday and Friday. And we don't have any ballet classes this week, but Abby said she was still going to dance with me to help me practice to get better. Do you think she'll dance with me all day on Wednesday since I don't have to go to school?"

Dean chuckled. "Abby works at the diner during the day, kiddo. I don't think she'll have the time."

"So am I going to have to work at the diner on Wednesday?"

He looked at her oddly. "No. Why would you think that?"

"Because she's my babysitter. And you have to work too." She took another bite of her cookie. "I have to stay some place if I'm not at school."

At that moment, Dean realized that he had taken for granted the fact that he'd have to discuss these things with her. From what he learned over the last couple of weeks, his sister never provided a particularly stable home life for the two of them and the last thing he wanted was for that pattern to continue.

"I'm going to work from home on Wednesday," he said, taking a bite of his own cookie.

"You can work from here? How come you don't do that all the time?"

"Sometimes I do, but the job I'm working on right now requires me to go into the office and work with a lot of other people. From now until after New Year's, though, I'll be working from home more. I'll be able to pick you up from the bus after school some more. Won't that be great?"

"But I go to ballet!" she cried.

He chuckled again. "Abby will still pick you up on ballet days. But on the days when you don't have a class and I'm working from home, I'll pick you up." He looked at her and couldn't help but grin as he watched her trying to work out all of this new information in her head.

"I like going to Abby's," Maya stated. "She's a fun ballet teacher and babysitter. I like her a lot."

"Me too."

"You should marry Abby!" she said excitedly. "Then I'd have a whole family like everyone else! Abby would be my new mom and you would be my new dad – even though you're my uncle. And then Abby could teach me to dance all the time!"

Dean nearly choked on the cookie and began to cough wildly. Maya patted him on the back to help him but it took several minutes for him to be able to breathe normally.

"Are you okay?" Maya asked when he finally stopped.

Nodding, he took a long drink from the glass of milk he'd poured earlier and scrambled to try to figure out how to respond to his niece's comment. He was used to her simply blurting out what was on her mind, but…this one was a little more shocking than anything she'd thrown out there before.

Putting his empty glass down, Dean looked at Maya.

And couldn't think of one word to say.

"So will you?" she asked excitedly. "Will you marry Abby?"

Crap. Now what?

"We could all live here and then maybe we could get a dog and I could name him Snuffles and he can sleep in my bed!" She stopped for a moment – Dean figured it was simply to catch her breath. "I hope he likes the cold because it's always cold here. I bet Abby will like Snuffles too and…"

"Maya!" Dean snapped, finally at his limit.

She looked at him – a little shocked at his tone.

He took a deep, steadying breath before speaking. "Maya…sweetheart…Abby and I aren't…I mean…"

"You like her, don't you?"

"I do," he began, "but people don't just rush off and get married because they like each other. At least…they shouldn't. I know you like Abby and she likes you too, but I don't want you getting your hopes up and planning on all these things, okay?"

Those big blue eyes filled with tears – but he was ready for them this time and swore they would not affect him.

"O-kay," she said quietly, her bottom lip quivering ever so slightly.

And now he felt like crap.

Maya finished her cookie and wiped her hands and mouth with a napkin. "May I be excused? I'm going to go play in my room now."

Dean couldn't have uttered a word even if he wanted to, so he simply nodded. With a sigh, he watched her walk from the room and wondered when he was going to get to the point where Maya's sadness and disappointment didn't feel like a kick in the gut.

He heard her bedroom door close and knew.

A long time.

****

Something was up.

All week long Abby felt like there was something wrong and she was determined to get to the bottom of it. It was Thanksgiving and Dean and Maya had just arrived and both seemed a little...subdued.

Just as they had all week.

She had been aware of Dean being able to work from home this week because of the holiday and with no dance classes scheduled, she didn't see Maya as much as she usually did, but when she did, the little girl was much quieter than usual. When Abby tried to find out if everything was all right, Maya simply shrugged and changed the subject.

And then there was Dean.

He had been sexy as all get-out every time she'd seen him, but he hadn't been particularly…attentive. She had a feeling it had to do with Maya and not wanting to do anything that might be considered inappropriate in front of her. While she completely understood the reasoning, it didn't mean that she didn't find the whole thing a little off-putting. After spending the night together, Abby had been looking forward to seeing Dean and being able to kiss him and touch him – in a completely appropriate way. Clearly that wasn't part of his plan because other than a distracted kiss on the cheek, he hadn't touched her at all since he left her house Sunday afternoon.

And that was completely unacceptable.

Dean carried in a couple of grocery bags and got things situated while Maya stood quietly by the kitchen table.

Yeah. Something was definitely up.

Rubbing her hands together, Abby asked, "Okay, who's ready to help me stuff the turkey?"

"Me! Me! Me!" Finally, Maya perked up.

"Excellent! I want you to go into the bathroom and wash your hands really well and dry them and then come back out here, okay?"

"Okay!" Maya cried excitedly right before she ran from the room.

Abby walked over and, without a word, cupped Dean's face in her hands and kissed him. She almost sagged with relief when he returned her kiss with the same passion. He hauled her close and she immediately wanted to wrap herself around him as his tongue tangled with hers. As much as she wanted to continue – to drag him down to the floor and have her way with him – she wanted answers more.

Reluctantly, she pulled her mouth from his and tried to catch her breath. "Okay. Good," she said breathlessly.

Dean looked at her funny.

"I was just making sure I hadn't imagined what happened Saturday night and Sunday morning," she said for clarification.

He still looked confused.

Sighing, Abby pulled out of his embrace and kept her voice low. "You've been very distant since Sunday. I'm sure some of it's because you don't want to do anything…inappropriate in front of Maya but…come on. You're treating me like I have the plague or something. So I just wanted to kiss you and see if…"

Dean held up a hand to stop her. "Okay, yeah. I got it." He sighed. "There was an awkward conversation on Sunday after I brought Maya home from Jenny's."

"What happened?"

He didn't get to elaborate because Maya came racing back into the room. "Look! My hands are super clean! I washed them three times! See?"

Abby smiled and complimented her on her great job. "Okay, let's get our aprons on and stuff this bird!"

The three of them worked together to get the meal prepped and the turkey in the oven. "I know this is all for a good cause, but I had no idea it was so much work!" she said, sitting down on the couch almost an hour later. Maya sat down beside her and Dean sat at the other end of the sofa, with his niece between them. Abby's mind raced with possibilities about what the awkward conversation could have possibly been, but for the life of her, she couldn't seem to settle on any one topic.

"What do we do while the turkey cooks?" Maya asked.

"Well, I was thinking we could either…watch a movie or…play a game," Abby said. "What do you think?"

"Can we do both? Can we watch a movie and then play a game?" Maya asked.

"Absolutely!" Grabbing the remote, Abby pulled up Netflix on the television and they searched through all of the children's movies until they found a Disney movie that Maya hadn't seen. Once it started, she got up and made some popcorn, grabbed drinks for everyone and, when she came back into the living room, she found

Maya on the floor propped up on some pillows. She looked at Dean curiously.

"She prefers to be on the floor for a movie," he said softly. His arm was stretched out along the back of the couch and Abby wasn't sure if that meant she could sit close to him or if she needed to keep her distance.

"Give me just one minute," she said and went back into the kitchen to put Maya's snack into her own bowl. She walked back and put the bowl on the floor next to her but Maya barely acknowledged Abby because she was already so engrossed in the movie.

When she turned toward the couch, Dean motioned for her to sit next to him and Abby's stomach fluttered. God, what was it about this man that had her feeling so…giddy? She was a grown woman and yet when Dean smiled at her, she felt like a teenage girl with her first crush! She thought she'd be more mature about it at this point in her life but Dean Hayes just had a way of making everything girly in her go on hyper-alert when he was near.

And that wasn't necessarily a bad thing.

As soon as she sat down, Dean wrapped an arm around her and pulled her close, tucking her in at his side. Abby felt his warm breath next to her ear. "I missed you."

*Oh thank God.* She didn't realize just how much she needed to hear that. As much as she wanted to turn and talk to him, the feel of his lips brushing her ear and his warm breath on her skin kept her exactly where she was.

"If it were up to me," Dean went on quietly, "I'd take you down the hall to your room, shut the door, and strip you down." His tongue traced the shell of her ear and Abby shivered with pleasure. "Then I'd lay you down on the bed and kiss every inch of you."

For a moment, Abby let herself wonder if Maya would even notice that they'd left the room.

"And after I had you crying out my name," he murmured for her ears only, "I'd get undressed and cover your body with mine so that we were skin-to-skin from head to toe."

She was panting. Literally, she sat there panting at his words.

"I'd have your hands in mine, pinned above your head. And then I'd take my time making love to you over and over again until we were both exhausted and too tired to move."

Oh God, did that sound wonderful. Once again, she looked over at Maya and then toward the hallway and wondered…

Dean chuckled lowly beside her. "Believe me, I wish," he said. "I've thought of it at least a hundred times this week."

Abby sagged and shifted until she could rest her head on his shoulder. "That was just mean," she whispered. "Telling me such a sexy story and then being responsible and telling me we can't do it."

"What are you doing tomorrow night?" he asked quietly.

A small smile played at her lips as she lifted her head and looked at him. "I have nothing planned."

"Maya's sleeping at Jenny's again. I was thinking you and I could have another sleepover too."

Her smile grew. "I like the way you think."

"And then on Saturday afternoon we're going out to pick out a Christmas tree. Maya's never had a real tree so we're going to make a day of it. We're going to get the tree and then I'm going to take her out to pick out some decorations of her own – you know, so she'll feel like it's her tree too. Then we'll have dinner and get the tree set in the stand."

"Are you going to decorate it that night?"

He shook his head. "I always let the tree settle for at least one night – let it get acclimated to the temperature in the house and all that before putting anything on it. It means staring at a bare tree for a day, but it's the way we've always done it."

"Us too. I normally get my tree this weekend too. Once Thanksgiving weekend is over, I'm so busy with rehearsals for the Christmas play that I don't have any other time to get one and decorate it. My mom and I almost always had a real tree and I remember hating to have to wait the extra day to let it settle in the stand. I imagine Maya's going to be a little impatient too. You'll have to let me know how she does."

Dean studied her for a long moment like he was trying to work something out in his head. Finally, he asked, "Would you like to join us?"

There was something in the way he asked. There was a hint of reluctance that had her feeling a little uncomfortable with readily accepting – which was what she really wanted to do. Putting a little space between them, Abby faced Dean. "Okay, what's going on?"

He frowned. "What do you mean?"

"What happened on Sunday?"

With a sigh, Dean shifted in his spot as well and hung his head, shaking it slightly before looking up at her again. "I guess at the sleepover the girls talked about their families. Their parents. Maya felt a little out of place and sad. She told me about it when we got home. Then she…well…she mentioned how much she likes spending time with you and then asked if I liked you and the next thing I know…she's making plans for us. As a family."

It took a minute for what he was saying to really sink in. Oh. *Oh!* "You mean…?"

He nodded. "She said we could get married and then she'd have a mom and a dad like everyone else. It just about killed me. She's too young to have to deal with all of this and I'm doing everything in my power to make sure she has everything she needs, but…"

Reaching out, Abby put her hand over his. "Dean, no one expects you to get married just to make your niece feel better. That's crazy."

He shook his head again and sighed. "I had no idea how to respond to her at first and then when I explained that…you know…you and I were…" He paused. "Anyway, she gave me the big sad eyes and quivering lip and then went to her room. I know some of that is a manipulation thing to get her way, but that time? It was genuine and it bothered me. So when we saw you during the week…"

"You didn't want to do anything to get her hopes up," Abby finished for him. Of course. Now it all made sense.

She moved a little bit farther away.

Dean held onto her hand and gently tugged her back toward him. "Abby…"

There were so many things she wanted to say, but now certainly wasn't the time. She wasn't exactly sure she could get into this with him with Maya sitting only a few feet away. While she knew Dean was going to have to face many challenges with his new role as a parent, she didn't want him thinking he had to make such a dramatic sacrifice for Maya's happiness. And even though Abby had grown up with a single parent, that parent was her biological mother. Maya didn't have that and as much as it broke her heart for the little girl, nothing Dean could do was going to change that.

But then another thought raced around her head.

*Marry Dean.*

Oh yeah…that had been part of her fantasy for a long time. Whenever Abby thought about getting married, she imagined Dean in the groom's role. Even when they didn't know each other beyond saying hello at the diner, she still held on to the silly dream.

If he asked her right now, she'd say yes. It wouldn't matter if he didn't love her; in time he would grow to. Wouldn't he? She had fallen in love with Dean Hayes a long time ago and it had only grown stronger once they started spending time together.

So yes, she'd marry him. Raise Maya with him.

And love every minute of it.

How crazy was that?

"You're looking pretty serious right now," Dean said, interrupting her thoughts. "What are you thinking?"

There was no way she could tell him that. So she fibbed a little. "I was thinking about all that food inside and hoping we timed it out right so it all comes out at the same time."

The look he gave said he didn't believe her, but he didn't say anything. Instead, he pulled her back and settled her beside him. She rested her head on his shoulder and smiled a little when he rested his head against hers. They held hands and both did their best to focus on the animated movie on the television.

Resting against him and breathing in, Abby could smell Dean's cologne and feel the heat of his body. A few feet away, Maya giggled at the song the characters were singing.

It was a good day.

And for now, that was more than enough.

# Eight

Thanksgiving had been a huge success, Dean thought the next day. They made way too much food but they enjoyed it and laughed and all in all, it had been a great day. He had agonized on whether or not to share with Abby his conversation with Maya regarding getting married, but in the end, it had been the right thing to do.

And in typical Abby form, she didn't seem the least bit shocked by it.

He just wasn't sure if he was relieved or not.

Hell, if he were honest, he'd admit that life would be a lot less stressful and complicated if he were married. There would be someone beside him to navigate this whole new phase with Maya. Someone who would share his fears and anxiety with. Someone who would understand that being thrown into the role of parenting was overwhelming and finally, someone who would tell him that it was all going to be all right and that it was normal to screw up once in a while.

*You already have that someone.*

*You're just not married to her.*

Okay, so there was that.

"So not the time," he murmured as he walked down the hall to Maya's room. She was packing up for her sleepover and they were running a little behind. "Hey, kiddo! You ready?"

"Yup!" She ran past him with her sleeping bag and a backpack full of toys. Dean picked up her little suitcase and turned off the light in her room before following her to the front door.

"Do you have everything?"

"Uh-huh!"

"Let's go," he said with a smile. Within minutes, they were in the car and heading down the road.

"Are we really going to go and get a Christmas tree tomorrow?" Maya asked with wonder.

"We sure are," he replied, smiling at her in the rear-view mirror.

"And I'm going to get to pick out my own decorations?"

"That's right!"

"And Abby's going to come with us?"

This had been the pattern. Even after he'd explained that he and Abby weren't getting married, Maya found a way to bring Abby's name into just about every conversation. "She is. She needs to get her tree this weekend too."

"How come?"

"Because next week starts the long rehearsals for the Christmas play so she won't have a lot of extra time." He paused. "You know she's going to be very busy for the next few weeks. So we have to be respectful of that so she can work and help all of her students get ready for the recital."

"I'm going to be in the recital too!" Maya said. "And next week I get to try on my costume and get it fitted."

"I'd ask if you're excited about it, but I can already tell that you are," Dean teased her and laughed when she started to giggle.

"Abby said that I have to remember to wear it only for the special rehearsals and for the recital and not when I'm at home," she said seriously. "But after the recital is done, I can wear it whenever I want."

Dean wasn't sure if he was actually supposed to respond to that, so he opted to stay quiet.

"Me and Jenny are going to practice our dance today. She's been taking ballet for two whole years so she's like a real ballerina. That's what I want to be, but I know I need more practice."

"I think you're doing a great job, kiddo. You've learned a lot in a few short weeks."

"That's because Abby's been helping me and giving me extra lessons. She's the best."

Dean simply nodded. He had a feeling with the good mood Maya was obviously in, if he gave even the slightest bit of praise to Abby, she'd jump all over it. It was just easier to keep quiet for now.

They pulled up to Jenny's house and being that they'd done this only a week before, it was fairly easy to drop Maya off and chat with Kathy and her husband for a few minutes before leaving. He kissed Maya goodbye and was out the door within ten minutes.

Once he pulled the car out of the driveway, he immediately headed to Abby's. Their time together was already so limited that he didn't want to waste any time. She knew what time he was dropping Maya off and she had mentioned she had another appointment to look at a building in downtown for the studio. They agreed he'd come over afterwards. With any luck, they'd be arriving at her house at the same time and he was beyond looking forward to seeing her.

Yesterday had been such a mixture of pleasure and pain. Well, maybe pain was a bit dramatic but…sitting with her on the couch and talking about all the things he'd wanted to do to her had done little more than tortured them both.

But he was planning on making up for it.

All day.

By the time he pulled up to Abby's house, he was beyond primed. Images of her sprawled out on the bed played on a continuous loop in his mind and Dean could only hope that he wasn't going to embarrass himself the moment he touched her.

He sprinted up her front steps and knocked on the door.

No answer.

He knocked again.

No answer.

Her car was in the driveway and she hadn't called or texted to say she was running late so where was she? Feeling a little concerned, he tried turning the knob and found the door unlocked. He stepped inside, closed the door and immediately called out to her.

"Abby? Abby, are you here?"

No answer.

He quickly scanned the living room and spotted her purse and keys, so where the hell was she? Dean made his way down the hall toward her bedroom, calling out to her the entire time.

At the door to her bedroom, he froze in his tracks.

There, sprawled out as if he'd put her there himself, was Abby. Wearing a sexy grin and little more than tiny pieces of red lace, she was his fantasy come to life.

Slowly he walked into the room. Stalked, actually. That was the primitive side of him, how he felt. She didn't move. She simply watched him approach.

"I was afraid you weren't coming," Abby whispered after a moment and Dean caught the double entendre.

"Sweetheart, trust me when I say that where you're concerned, that's never going to be a problem."

****

Being sexually aggressive was never Abby's thing. She'd never particularly wanted to be, but ever since Dean whispered in her ear about all the things he wanted to do to her, she could barely think of anything else!

And while she had tossed around the idea of answering the door and leading him down the hall, this scenario came to mind and she decided to just go for it. Judging by the look of raw desire on Dean's face, she'd say she made the right choice.

Wordlessly, he undressed – his eyes intently fixed on hers the entire time. Abby could feel the heat from his gaze and it took a lot of self-control not to squirm or look away. And really, looking away was not an option. Dean fully dressed was sexy enough, but once he took his shirt off and she could see his muscled arms and chest and torso? Sexy wasn't even a strong enough word to describe him

He was down to nothing but his jeans when he placed his knee on the bed and reached out to run his hands up her calves and over her knees. Dean's hands were large and slightly rough and it felt so damn good that Abby couldn't help but let out a low moan.

"I believe I mentioned kissing every inch of you," he said, his voice low and thick and Abby could feel herself trembling in anticipation. Lowering his head, Dean began to do just that.

He started by kissing her ankles and then slowly made his way up one shin and then the other. Between the warmth of his breath, the glide of his tongue and his hands moving along her skin, Abby was fairly certain she was going to go up in flames. She was breathless and hot and Dean seemed to be taking great pleasure in going slowly to make sure he covered every inch of her.

*Damn the man*, she thought.

Unable to help herself, she began to whimper, beg, plead and cry out his name. He kissed her hip bone before saying, "Patience."

Easy for him to say.

"I promise to have patience later," she said breathlessly. "But right now, I'd really love it if you moved on to the next phase."

He chuckled and sat up slightly. "The next phase?"

Abby nodded and licked her lips. "The getting naked phase. Please."

For a minute, he didn't move. He didn't do much of anything besides watch her intently. She squirmed under him as he straddled her.

Slowly he unbuttoned his jeans and lowered the zipper. He didn't move off of her. Instead Dean shifted so he was stretched out on top of her – chest to chest, skin to skin and Abby almost wept with how good he felt. She loved the feel of his weight on top of her. Wrapping her legs around his waist, she pulled him a little bit closer.

"Hard for me to get naked when you've got those fantastic legs locked around me," he murmured against her neck where he'd begun to lick and nip and kiss.

Using the heels of her feet, Abby began to work on lowering his jeans over his hips. She only got them to move a little before Dean jumped up and took them and his boxers off himself.

And then he was back – covering her body with his – and it was so damn glorious that Abby let out a very contented sigh. "That is *so* much better."

"Almost," he said, going back to that spot on her neck that he'd just vacated.

Abby arched her back under him at the same time Dean reached beneath her to unclasp her bra. They worked together to get it off and she let out a small laugh when he flung it across the room. He laughed with her and she was certain her panties would be next, but instead Dean lowered his head to her breasts and began to give them the same attention he'd been giving to other parts of her body.

He was clearly trying to kill her.

But it felt so damn good that she couldn't find the strength to care or protest.

Raking her hands up into his hair, Abby held Dean to her – keeping her back arched at the same time and simply letting him have his way with her.

Because he was really good at it.

It could have been minutes. It could have been hours, but all Abby knew was that it was too long. Too much. Too intense. And he hadn't even kissed her properly yet. With a slight tug on his hair, she got him to look up at her. He had a cocky grin on his face and it should have irked her, but all she could think of was how long she had dreamed of having Dean look at her like that.

Turned on.

By her.

"I need you," she finally said. Playtime was over. She couldn't take anymore. Foreplay was a wonderful thing and they'd been having the mental version since the day before. It was time to take action and get to what she knew they both craved.

Rearing up, Dean ran a hand from Abby's shoulder and down over her breasts and her belly before settling on the red lace of her panties. She quivered in anticipation. Staring at where his hand was, Dean studied that spot for a moment before meeting her eyes again.

"I promise to buy you a new pair," he said huskily right before ripping the lace from her body.

Abby let out a squeal of delight before pulling him down for the kiss she'd been waiting all day for.

****

"So I was thinking," Abby began much later, "that maybe we could go out and get my tree tonight so that it's here and set up and then you and Maya can do your thing tomorrow."

They were still in bed and Dean was enjoying having her sprawled out partially on top of him. "Why? I thought you wanted to go with us."

"I do, but I thought it might be better for the two of you to do it together without me and maybe make this the start of a new tradition. I'd be a distraction."

He had to agree. Her naked body was distracting the hell out of him right now. "I thought we had it all worked out. We were going to pick Maya up together and go and get both the trees, bring them back to each of our houses and then go shopping for ornaments before grabbing dinner. Maya's really looking forward to it."

And to be honest, so was he.

Abby raised her head and smiled softly at him. "I know she is, but after what you shared with me about how she's viewing the three of us, I sort of think that maybe…I just don't want to confuse her, Dean." She paused. "You know I love spending time with the two of you but she's dealing with enough upheaval and changes in her life, I don't want to add to that."

Even though she was saying everything that he had said to himself in the last week, it didn't sit right with him. "I know what you're saying," he began carefully, "but I think it's also important for Maya to realize that she can't always get her way by crying or pouting or…giving me the silent treatment. The fact is that you are an important part of our lives and we enjoy spending time with you too. Maybe by spending time together and reinforcing that…"

He stopped. That what? That they could do stuff like a family without actually being one? Was that really what he wanted to say?

"I know what you're saying," Abby quickly interrupted, but he couldn't tell if she was offended or upset by where he was going.

Rolling them over until Abby was on her back and he was looking down at her, Dean studied her face. She didn't look upset, but…hell. He was.

"Look, I don't know what I'm doing half the time. Everything where Maya is concerned has been nothing but trial and error. And I find that I'm spending a lot of my time kicking my own ass because I wasted so much time…so much of my life…not living!"

"Dean…"

"No, I'm serious," he interjected. "I used to go into the diner every damn day. Do you know why?"

"Dan makes really good pancakes?" she offered with an attempt at humor.

Unfortunately, Dean couldn't help but chuckle. "No," he said after a minute. "I went in there every day to try to feel normal. To try to interact with people because I was lonely. I went in there to see *you*."

He hadn't intended to share that, but…there it was.

Abby's eyes went wide. "You…you did?  But…I didn't think that you…I mean…"

Leaning down, he kissed her softly on the lips before lifting his head again.  "I know.  I was kind of in denial.  I'm good at that."  Then he shook his head and sighed.  "For so damn long I separated myself from everyone – from doing things that I enjoyed  because I didn't want anyone to compare me to my sister.  She was always in some kind of trouble and I knew that everyone was just waiting for me to do the same."

"Then why did you stay?  Wouldn't it have been easier to move someplace else and just start over?"

"Maybe.  But I love Silver Bell Falls.  This is where I grew up and it's where I always envisioned I'd raise my own family.  I refused to let other people's prejudices take that away from me."

"But you did," Abby replied.  "Even though you stayed here, you weren't allowing yourself to get involved in anything or to live a normal life."

"I know."

"And I hate to say it, Dean, but those same people are still going to be watching you.  And now they're watching both you and Maya.  They're going to wonder if she's got a wild streak like her mom.  I hate that for her, but that's what goes with small-town life."

"Damn, I hadn't even thought of that.  The last thing I want is anyone to put a label on Maya or to compare her to Karen.  That's not fair.  I know Karen was her mother and I certainly don't want Maya to forget her, but I also don't want anyone talking badly about her in front of Maya. Does that make sense?"

She nodded. "Of course it does! I'd hope that people wouldn't be that cruel. And it has been a long time since your sister lived here. I just hope that people will look at Maya and see a sweet little girl who is trying to figure out her new life here with her uncle."

They were both quiet for a long moment.

"I think she's doing okay," Dean said quietly. "Don't you?"

His dark eyes looked at Abby with a hint of desperation. "I do," she agreed. "In these last few weeks I've noticed so many changes in her. She's always been sweet and friendly and outgoing, but the longer she's here, the more confident she's become."

"I want to make this Christmas special for her. Not that I want to spoil her or bribe her with presents, but…I like what you said earlier about us starting some new traditions."

"It's going to be wonderful, Dean. That's why I don't want to interfere. Years from now, I want you to be able to look back on this Christmas and have memories of each other and not…you know…someone else horning in on it."

Did she really believe that there would be a time when all she would be is a random person in their memories?  Didn't she realize how much she meant to them?  To him?

Of course she didn't.  They had only been involved for less than a month and even though they'd known each other for much longer, for all intents and purposes, it was too soon to think about the future.

Wasn't it?

"I'll make you a deal," he said.

"O-kay…"

"We'll go out tonight and find you a tree, bring it back here and put it in a stand to let it do its thing."

"And…"

"And then we'll come back in here and go for round two," he said with a lecherous wink.

Abby giggled and tried to push him off of her, but Dean wouldn't budge.

"I was thinking we could grab a bite to eat before we get the tree," he went on.  "And then tomorrow – after a late breakfast in bed – we'll go together to pick up Maya and go on with our original plan."

"Dean…"

He placed a finger over her lips.  "I'm serious, Abby.  Maya and I both want you with us for this.  It's supposed to snow a little tomorrow and we'll bring a big thermos of hot chocolate with us. It's going to be awesome.  Please?  Please say you'll come with us."

Her expression was serious as she looked up at him. "I have one condition."

Relief immediately washed over him. "Anything. Name it."

"You make the breakfast," she said as a slow smile spread across her face.

"I can make toast," he said, trying hard to hide a grin.

"As long as you serve it to me in bed, I'm okay with that."

Laughing out loud, Dean hugged her close and rolled them over again so that Abby was straddling him. "I don't know about you, but I think I could go for round two now. How about we go for round three after we get back."

Licking her lips, Abby nodded. "As usual, I really like the way you think."

\*\*\*\*

"So are you one of those people who likes to look and touch every tree on the lot or are you more the kind who just sees it and knows?" Dean asked later that evening.

They were walking hand in hand through the Christmas tree lot. They were getting a lot of curious stares but neither seemed to notice. The air was cold, but they didn't notice that either as they made their way around.

"I think I'm a little bit of both," Abby replied, taking in all of the trees around them. "Sometimes I'll walk onto a lot and see a tree and just think, 'Yes! That's it!' Other times I'm not overly impressed and so I start digging through the rows and checking them all out. Normally, I have good luck at this lot. Ruth and Jim really produce some great trees every year."

Dean nodded. "This is where I usually come to get my tree too. I think it's still early enough that we'll have a good selection to choose from for Maya."

Chuckling, Abby nudged him with her shoulder. "You'll be here in less than twenty-four hours. I doubt they're going to have a big rush on trees before then."

"You never know," Dean teased. "There are a lot of people out shopping tonight."

"You'd think they'd be shopped out since it's Black Friday. I would have thought everyone would be at home sleeping after getting up and hitting the malls so early in the morning."

"You sound like you've been there and done that yourself."

She shook her head. "Not in a long time. I'll still go out and shop for a few things but the majority of my Christmas shopping is done online because I don't have a lot of free time this time of year. Plus, my list is fairly small. It's just me and my mom and a few friends."

And this year she'd have Dean and Maya to shop for too, she thought to herself, and it made her smile.

"That reminds me," she went on, "has Maya added anything else to her Christmas list yet?"

Dean stopped in his tracks and stared at her. "Was she supposed to?"

"I just thought she would. When we talked about it that night we baked cookies, she only had a few things on it. I figured with her making friends and settling in a little bit more that she'd find more stuff to ask for."

"Is that something I should ask her about?"

That had her chuckling. "I would have thought she shared it with you already. I know when I was growing up my Christmas list was done before Thanksgiving – or it was supposed to be! But I was continually adding stuff to it right up until…" And then she stopped and caught herself. "Sorry. I'm sure with everything going on…with losing her mother and the move…I'm sure it's the last thing on her mind."

"Mine too," he murmured.

They walked along and Abby couldn't help but feel sad for both Maya and Dean. This would be a difficult Christmas for the both of them. Nothing she could do was going to make up for their loss – and she certainly wasn't going to even pretend to try – but she did want to do something to make it special for them.

"Are your parents coming for Christmas?" she asked.

"No. They really can't stand the cold weather anymore. Once they got a taste of the warm winter temperatures in the South, they vowed to stay where they were. They'd gone to Karen's for Maya's first few Christmases, but then they stopped. And I would go to her house as well because…" He stopped and shrugged. "We were all each other had."

"At least Maya's close to you and you already have the tradition of spending Christmas together. Now you get to change it up a bit and make it your own."

"I have no idea how to do that."

His honesty twisted her heart.

Squeezing his hand, she moved a little bit closer to him as they walked. "You could make a special meal for Christmas Eve and Christmas Day. Have a special breakfast that you'll only ever have on Christmas morning. You can bake cookies that are only for Santa...I know my mom and I have a ton of Christmas-related traditions and even when she's not here, I still do them."

She was about to elaborate but she couldn't.

She found her tree.

Stopping, Abby pointed and Dean looked in that direction and smiled. "That's the one, huh?"

Nodding, Abby pulled her hand from his and walked over to the six-foot Fraser fir. She touched it and smelled it as she walked around it, smiling the entire time. Yes, this was her tree. "It's perfect."

Dean walked off to get one of the attendants to help them and within minutes, the tree was getting trimmed, wrapped and loaded onto the top of his car. Abby was practically bouncing on her toes. She loved this. The cold, the carols, the smell of pine in the air…and now…Dean standing beside her keeping her warm.

"You ready?" he asked as the attendant wished them a good night.

"Did you see any that you were interested in?"

"I did, but I want to let Maya pick out the tree tomorrow on her own. I don't want to bring her here and guide her. I want this to be something she gets to do and can be excited about." He laughed quietly. "I guess that can be our first new tradition."

The sheepish look on his face was so sweet and adorable that Abby couldn't help herself. She came around to the driver's side of the car and kissed him.

When she moved back, he was smiling at her. "What was that for?"

"Because you're amazing."

His dark eyes went wide. "Seriously?"

She nodded. "You are. I think that you are off to a very good start on the Christmas traditions and you're going to make some great ones as you go."

He looked at her as if he didn't quite believe her. "I wish I had your confidence."

"That's okay because I have enough for the both of us. Now let's go home and get this tree inside and I'll make us some hot chocolate."

Before she could move, Dean reached for her hand and tugged her back in for a longer kiss. "Hot chocolate sounds good, but I believe we discussed another round earlier."

*Oh my.*

She snuggled closer and almost purred. "I believe you're right. Maybe we can combine the two."

Dean kissed her one more time. It was hotter and wetter than the last one and if they weren't in public, she'd be all over him.

"Let's get you home," he murmured against her lips. "And maybe we'll come up with a new tradition or two for celebrating finding a Christmas tree."

She was definitely on board with that. With a small giggle, she pulled free and ran around to her side of the car and climbed in, giddy with anticipation.

# Nine

"Soooo…I can pick any tree that's here?" Maya asked the next afternoon, shouting to be heard over the Christmas carol that was playing loudly over the sound system. It was even colder than it was the previous night and snow flurries were blowing around.

"That's right," Dean said, silently praying that she'd find a tree quickly so they could get out of the cold.

"But there are so many! How am I supposed to pick just one?"

Beside her, Abby crouched down. "Do you want to know how I pick my tree?"

Maya nodded.

"I always want one that is really green and really fat. I check to make sure there are no big gaps in the branches and no brown spots. And then I try to picture how he'll look in the corner of my living room."

"He?" Maya asked, her brows scrunched in confusion.

Abby giggled. "I always think of my Christmas tree as a he. I don't really know why, but I always do."

"Oh," Maya replied seriously. She looked up at Dean. "Do you think the tree is a he?"

"Uh…"

"It doesn't really matter," Abby said cheerily. "Let's start looking around and we'll look for all the important things." Then she turned to Dean. "Where do you put your tree?"

"In the corner of the living room between the window and the TV," he replied. "I tend to go more for a tall tree. I have ten-foot ceilings so we have the space for up to a nine foot tree."

"Wow," Maya said. "That's like a giant tree!"

"Well…let's go find you a giant tree then!" Abby said, taking her by the hand and leading her toward the first row of trees.

Dean stood back for a moment and simply watched. The snow was falling, and even though they were all bundled up, Maya's cheeks were rosy. Her eyes were wide with excitement as she listened to everything Abby said. He could hear them laughing and then observed as they stopped at one tree and began inspecting it while discussing the pros and cons.

They were making a memory.

A tradition.

A tradition that he was missing because he was too busy standing back and enjoying watching them! Clearing his head, Dean caught up to where they were standing and chatting. "So, what the verdict on this one?"

"He's very green," Maya said diplomatically.

"And he smells wonderful," Abby added.

"Hmm…" Dean said, pausing to inspect the tree himself. "I think we can go a little taller. This one's only about seven feet tall."

"Yeah! A bigger one!" Maya cried out excitedly. "Where are the bigger ones?"

Dean pointed toward the end of the row. "The taller ones are usually in the back. Let's go check them out, okay?"

Maya skipped ahead of them and while she did, Dean took one of Abby's hands in his and squeezed it.

"I think she's having a great time," Abby said as they walked along. "She's taking it all very seriously so I'm pretty sure you're going to end up with a great tree."

"I wasn't worried about that. I just want Maya to feel like she's a part of the whole holiday and…the tradition."

Abby smiled at him. "You're a good uncle."

"Thanks." They found Maya standing in front of a long row of really tall Christmas trees. In comparison, she looked even smaller than usual. Dean walked over to her and crouched down beside her. "What do you think? Any good ones?"

"I don't know," she said, looking around. "They're all really big."

"How about…we do this?" Dean scooped Maya up and sat her on his shoulders. She laughed hysterically as he got her situated. "What do you think? Does this help?"

"This is awesome! I'm as tall as the trees! Look at me, Abby! I'm as tall as the trees!"

"Wow! You are super tall right now!" Abby said with a laugh. "You'll be able to find all the good ones from up there!"

"Yeah!"

Together, they walked around and looked at just about every tree that was taller than eight feet and in the end, it was the very last tree on the lot that they deemed to be perfect.

"I need to get down, Uncle Dean! I need to see the bottom part of it too!"

He lowered his niece to the ground and then stood back with Abby and watched her do the final inspection.

Finally, Maya looked at the two of them and nodded. "Yup. This is the one. This is our tree! Can we get it? Can we take it home now?"

"Absolutely," Dean said. The snow was coming down harder and he motioned for one of the clerks to come and help them. He picked Maya up and held her close to keep her warm.

"Maybe we should go and wait in the car and have some hot chocolate," Abby suggested.

"But I want to see what they do to the tree to get him ready!" Maya cried. "Can we have the hot chocolate out here while they work on him?"

Chuckling, Abby nodded. Dean handed her the keys to the car and watched as she walked away.

"Abby's the best!" Maya said and Dean was a little too engrossed in watching Abby walk away to think before he spoke.

"She certainly is."

"And she's really pretty…"

"Beautiful," he murmured.

Maya tightened her grip on him and hugged him, then kissed him soundly on the cheek. Dean pulled back to look at her and couldn't help but smile. "What was that for?"

"Because you're the best and we found the best tree and it's snowing and…and…it's the best day ever!"

"That's a lot of bests," he said, and tapped her gently on the nose. "Let's go and watch our tree get trimmed so we can get in the car and warm up!"

"Okay!"

They walked up to the front of the lot where they watched as the attendant cut the tree back a little and then wrapped it. Abby joined them and they each drank a small mug of hot chocolate as they waited. Unable to help himself, Dean pulled Abby in close so they were all huddled together. He tried telling himself it was for warmth, but he knew he was only partially lying to himself. It just felt good to have her near. He loved the feel of her beside him, loved being able to simply reach out and touch her.

"Dean?"

He turned and realized Abby was speaking to him. "Huh?"

"You zoned out there for a minute. Bill asked if you wanted help tying the tree to the car," she said patiently, smiling.

"Oh…uh…sure. Yes. Thanks." He stepped away from Abby and Maya to help get the tree secured to the car. Ten minutes later, they were all warmly ensconced in the heated car and heading toward home."

"Are we going to go and get my ornaments now?" Maya asked.

Dean knew he had promised, but the snow was really starting to come down. "We need to take the tree home and get it in the house and into a stand first. Then we'll need to see how the snow is doing. It's not safe to be out driving in it for too long."

Then he braced himself for the pouting and disappointment that usually followed when Maya didn't get her way, but surprisingly, she simply said okay and let it go. He mentally shook his head because just when he thought he had her figured out, she did the unexpected.

The drive home was hampered slightly by the weather but it didn't do anything for Maya's mood. She chatted on and on about the tree and the kind of decorations she wanted to get for it and how she couldn't wait to put presents under it.

Dean carried the tree into the house and set it in the stand he'd put out earlier. Abby and Maya stood back as he worked. After Dean cut the netting off of the tree and the branches started to unfold, they all agreed that it was going to be a beauty.

Maya ran over to the window and sighed. "It's still snowing hard."

"I know, kiddo, and I'm sorry. I promise that we'll go out tomorrow and get those decorations. We won't put one thing on this tree until you have ones of your own, okay?"

She nodded. "Is it going to snow all day?"

He walked over to the window and looked out with her. "I think so. We'll be snowed in tonight but the plows will come through in the morning and clear the roads so we should be okay to go out tomorrow after lunch. I'm sorry, Maya."

"It's okay," she said with another sigh. "Can we build a snowman? Sheriff Stone said you can build good snowmen here."

Dean remembered that conversation. "There's not enough snow out there yet but later on we probably could. Definitely tomorrow."

Maya turned and looked at Abby. "Will you build a snowman with me later?"

Abby looked at Dean first and he knew what she was thinking. The snow was coming down hard and fast and she was going to need to go home. Sooner rather than later.

Damn.

****

Sure there had been the weather warnings. Abby heard and watched them all morning and yet…she still went out with Dean and Maya to get a Christmas tree. This was Silver Bell Falls. Snow was the norm in the wintertime and didn't keep her from doing the things she wanted to do.

Her car wasn't that great in the snow but she'd driven in worse conditions.

Maybe.

Once or twice.

Okay, once and she got stuck and had to walk a mile home in a blizzard. Not something she wanted to do again, but how could she have missed going hunting for a Christmas tree with them? Seeing Maya's face as they looked around and when they found the tree was priceless!

Unfortunately, now she had to leave or she wasn't sure her car would get her home. The look on Dean's face told her that he understood, but Maya's was a completely different story.

And then there was the surprise she had planned…

Damn snow.

"I promise to come back and build one with you before we go shopping tomorrow," Abby said carefully. "But…I really need to get home now."

"But wait!" Maya cried, stepping away from the window. "You can't leave! The roads aren't safe! Uncle Dean said so!" She looked up at Dean and tugged at his hand. "Tell her! Tell Abby that it's not safe to drive!"

Abby watched the indecision on Dean's face and decided to put an end to it. "It's okay. Really. I don't live that far away and if I leave now, I'm sure I'll be fine."

"Abby, I hate to say it but…Maya has a point. The roads were slick when we were driving home here. And they're going to be worse now and you…well…you don't have good tires on your car."

Granted, Abby knew that but she hated that Dean noticed it too. "They're not so bad and really, if I leave now…"

"I'd feel really bad if something happened while you were driving," he said, a small smile tugging at his lips. "You should stay here."

Damn the man. That was what she wanted more than anything but it wasn't right with Maya in the house.

"We could have a sleepover!" Maya cried happily. "We can put a fire in the fireplace and sleep out here or we can all sleep in Uncle Dean's bed because it's really big and we can have popcorn and watch movies and…"

"Easy, Maya," Dean said softly, even as he chuckled. Then he looked at Abby. "I think a sleepover could be fun."

Double damn the man.

"Dean…"

"Strictly platonic," he said softly as he moved closer to her, his smile growing. Turning to Maya he said, "Why don't you go and see how many packs of popcorn we have?"

"Okay!" she agreed and then ran for the kitchen.

Dean stepped in even closer to Abby. "Now you'll get to sleep at my house."

She laughed softly. "I didn't bring my pajamas."

He groaned low and deep. "Any other time that wouldn't be a problem, but I think we can find something for you to wear tonight."

Tilting her head, she studied his handsome face. "Actually, I have a change of clothes out in the car. I may need a t-shirt or something, but I have some leggings and stuff that I can change into."

His eyes narrowed slightly. "Do you always travel with a change of clothes or was it wishful thinking?"

"Wishful thinking?"

Completely closing the distance between them, Dean placed his hands on Abby's hips, pulling her flush against him. "That you'd have to stay here tonight."

"Mmm…" she purred. "It had crossed my mind, but I'm afraid that I'll have to crush your fantasy. I carry a change of clothes with me all the time. Between the diner and dance classes, I never know if I'll need something to change into for whatever reason."

"Oh." Disappointment laced his tone. "Well that sucks."

"Not really. It's coming in handy for tonight."

"Maybe."

Sighing, Abby rested her head on his chest. "But we will have to think about the sleeping arrangements for tonight. I don't want to add any fuel to Maya's fire where we're concerned."

"I'm not worried about that."

"You're not?" she asked, confused.

He didn't answer. Instead he placed a kiss on the top of her head and stepped away. "I'm going to check on Maya."

For a minute, Abby was too confused to move. What changed that suddenly he was more comfortable with their relationship and how it looked in front of

Maya? Dean hadn't mentioned anything to her and, up until just now, she thought they were still acting casually in front of her.

"We have lots of popcorn!" Maya called out.

Deciding to let it go, Abby walked toward the kitchen and decided to share her own surprise with them. "Ooh…I do love popcorn. You know what else is great on a snowy day?"

Maya's eyes widened. "What?"

"Freshly-baked cookies," Abby said with a grin.

"But…but we don't have the stuff for that," Maya said, her brows scrunching up. "We used it all when we baked the cookies last time."

Abby's grin widened as she walked over to Dean's pantry. "Earlier, while the two of you were getting your shoes on, I snuck these supplies in." She reached in, pulled out two grocery bags and held them up. "We have enough here for chocolate chip cookies, sugar cookies, oatmeal raisin cookies and peanut butter cookies!"

"Yeah!" Maya cheered. "We can eat cookies all weekend!"

Putting the bags on the counter, Abby looked at Dean and Maya. "I really hoped that the weather forecast was wrong and that we'd have fun baking cookies just because we wanted to and not because we're stuck inside in a snowstorm." She shrugged. "I wanted it to be a surprise for when we got back from getting the new ornaments."

Dean stepped forward and hugged her. Abby's heart melted just a little bit. "Thank you," he murmured in her ear. "You're amazing."

Abby stepped out of his embrace and sheepishly looked at the two of them again. "Actually, I have one more surprise."

"You do?" Maya asked.

"Really?" Dean asked with a small laugh. "Is it better than homemade cookies?"

Laughing with him, she looked over at Maya. "Well, I think it may be better for one of us." Then she looked at Dean. "Would you mind going out to my car? My gym bag is on the back seat and then there's another bag back there. Could you bring them both in?"

He didn't question her, he simply nodded and did as she asked.

Taking Maya by the hand, Abby led her back out to the living room and sat them both down on the couch. "When I was growing up, my mom always got me a new Christmas ornament every year. At first there was a theme – baby's first Christmas, second Christmas and so on until I was five. Then she would get ornaments that were about something going on in my life or something that she knew was a favorite of mine."

"Like what?" Maya asked curiously.

"Well, there were Disney ornaments with some of my favorite characters and there were ballet-themed ornaments to celebrate my dance accomplishments." She paused. "Sometimes it was just a fun ornament with my name on it. And now I have a lot of those ornaments to put on my tree. My mom kept a lot of them so she can still put them on her tree but... every year when I decorate and I look at those ornaments, they make me smile."

"We never had a big tree," Maya said quietly, studying her hands that were folded in her lap. "I only ever helped decorate the tree once. I was too small before that, I guess. But we didn't have any stories with our ornaments. They were just colored balls." She shrugged. "No big deal."

"Oh, I don't know about that," Abby said, placing an arm around the girl. "We used to have some of those on our tree too and even though they were plain, they still had a story."

"They did?"

Abby nodded. "Uh-huh! We bought those the year I turned six. That was the year my mom decided that I was old enough to have a big tree that we could decorate. Before that, we had a small one that she would put on a table so I wouldn't touch it."

"My mom did that too."

"I think it's a mom thing," Abby said lightly. "They try to protect us from getting hurt."

Maya didn't say anything. She just nodded.

Dean walked back into the house and put Abby's gym bag down before walking over to them and handing her the other bag. It was a red gift bag with white tissue paper sticking out and Abby immediately handed it to Maya.

"This is for you."

Maya carefully took the bag as if it were something fragile and then slowly pulled the tissue paper out. When she reached inside, she looked at Abby before she pulled out. There was a mixture of excitement and uncertainty on her sweet little face and Abby had a feeling Maya hadn't been on the receiving end of too many happy surprises.

Putting the bag aside, Maya slowly unwrapped the ball of tissue paper and then gasped. "It's a ballerina ornament!" She said it so softly and with such wonder that Abby knew she'd made the right decision.

"And see, she's wearing all pink and has blonde hair just like you," Abby said, bending down to point out some of the details. "I thought she would make a great addition to your ornament collection so that you'll always remember the first Christmas that you learned ballet."

In the blink of an eye, Maya wrapped around Abby, hugging her tightly. Abby's arms immediately went around her as she willed herself not to cry. It was such a simple gift and it clearly meant a lot to Maya and for that, Abby was pleased.

And choked up.

Beside them, Dean cleared his throat. Maya gave her one more squeeze before pulling back. Then she held out the ornament for Dean to see.

"Look, Uncle Dean! It's me!"

Smiling, Dean sat down beside her and looked at it. "It sure is, kiddo," he said, placing a soft kiss on the top of her head. "And tomorrow, I think that should be the very first ornament we put on the tree. What do you think?"

"I can't wait!"

It felt good. Abby quietly congratulated herself on finding something that was meaningful for Maya because she knew it would be something she'd always remember. Abby knew if she sat here much longer thinking about it, she'd start crying for sure.

She was a sucker for sentimental stuff.

"What do you say we go and get our baking supplies set up?" she said as a distraction, standing up. "We can get in a couple of hours of baking before dinnertime."

Dean suggested that Maya go and wash up and once she was out of the room, he pulled Abby into his arms and rested his forehead against hers. "Thank you."

Even though she kind of suspected what he was thanking her for, she couldn't help but want to hear it. "For what?"

He smiled. "You totally saved the day. I really thought the snow would hold off a little longer and that we'd get to do all of the things we'd planned on. I knew Maya was going to be disappointed and bored about being snowed in, but somehow you managed to fix it all. You're amazing."

Snuggling close to him, Abby hid her smile against his chest. "Well, I just thought the baking would be a good distraction since the tree needs to acclimate to being indoors. I had a feeling Maya would be anxious about decorating and thought baking would help shift her focus."

"And then the ornament," he said.

She shrugged, still not looking up at him. "I saw it when I was out shopping the other day and it reminded me of her. I used to love when my mom got me personalized ornaments. I thought Maya probably would too." Then she mentally cursed. "I mean…obviously I'm not her mom but…"

"I know what you meant, Abby," he replied softly. "And it was a very thoughtful thing to do. You made her day."

"I don't know about that…"

"Are you kidding?" He tucked a finger under her chin and gently forced her to look at him. "Between the cookies and the ballerina, trust me. You made her day."

"Thanks." Pausing, Abby decided that they didn't have a lot of time before Maya came back into the room and she did need to ask him some questions. "What are we doing about the sleeping arrangements tonight? I don't think it's a good idea for me to sleep with you when Maya's here. It's not...I don't know...it doesn't seem..."

He placed a finger over her lips. "I know. And I also know this wasn't planned so you can take my bed and I'll sleep out here on the couch."

"You must think I'm being ridiculous..."

Shaking his head, Dean held her chin and said, "I think you are completely selfless. I see all that you do for everyone and how you put everyone else and their needs before your own. And I have to admit, I kind of like that you're worried about how it will look to my five-year-old niece if we sleep together." He placed a quick kiss on the tip of her nose. "That's not to say that I like the situation because believe me, I would really like to sleep with you in my bed. We wouldn't have to do anything but...just thinking about holding you all night was something I was looking forward to."

And really, so was she.

Sometimes being the responsible one sucked.

Like right now.

Sighing, Abby gave him a quick hug and just as she stepped out of his embrace, Maya came running back into the room.

"I'm ready! I'm ready! I'm ready!" she cried, grinning from ear to ear. "Can we make the chocolate chip ones first? And then can we have them for dessert?"

"We can definitely make them first," Abby said, "but it's up to your uncle what we have for dessert."

The look on Dean's face told her exactly what he wanted for dessert and Abby could feel herself blush.

"I think we can do that," Dean said. "We don't have anything major planned for dinner. I thought we were going to be out shopping so I planned to grab something in town, but now…"

Abby held up her hand. "Let's go and see what you have and we'll make this entire night a culinary adventure!"

"What's a culin…a cul…nary…," Maya sighed dramatically. "What's that?"

"That means food. We're going to have a food adventure!" she said excitedly. "We're going to go into the kitchen and raid the refrigerator and cabinets and see what we can come up with. Maybe it will be sandwiches, maybe it will be soup or…"

"No casseroles!" Dean and Maya called out and they all laughed.

Nodding, Abby laughed with them. "Got it. No casseroles. Now let's go!"

# Ten

For dinner, they ate soup and grilled cheese sandwiches in front of the fire, not by choice, but because they'd lost power. Luckily, all of the cookies had been baked and Abby had barely gotten the last grilled cheese out of the pan when the lights went out. Maya had been mildly upset by the whole thing, but once the fire was going she seemed to calm down.

They finished cleaning up and there wasn't much else they could do without power.

"Can we sleep out here?" Maya asked. "So we can be warm?"

He'd pulled out flashlights and they had plenty of firewood so they were basically good. There had been many storms where he'd lost power and it really wasn't anything to get so worked up about, but he was. For years he'd been telling himself to get a generator. Not the small gasoline one he had in his garage, but a real one that kicked on as soon as the power went out. But he never did – mainly because it was always just him and it hadn't been a big deal. Now with a child in the house, he was realizing that it would have been a smart thing to have.

"Do you have extra blankets or sleeping bags?" Abby asked. "We can make this whole area our camp so that we're all close to the fire."

Nodding, he grabbed a flashlight and stalked off down the hall to get what she requested. Behind him, Dean heard Abby helping Maya to her room to get her sleeping bag and pillow.

"Okay, you've got your flashlight," Abby said. "Do you need help getting into your pajamas?"

"It's still early," Maya said and Dean could hear the pout in her voice. "Why do I have to put them on now?"

"Because we're all going to be going to bed early. There's no power and not much else to do. I know we have your uncle's laptop so maybe we can watch a movie if he has one downloaded on it, but if not, sleep is really the only thing we can do."

"Darn. I wanted to have cookies and milk too."

"Tell you what, Maya Papaya," Abby began. "You get into your pajamas and help us get our camp set up and we'll all have cookies and milk before we go to bed, okay?"

"O-kay!"

Dean supposed she was doing what Abby asked and he was relieved. Pulling open his linen closet, he reached for some extra blankets when he heard Abby come up behind him. He glanced at her over his shoulder before going back to his task.

"Are you all right?"

He shrugged. "Sure. Why wouldn't I be?"

"That's what I'm wondering. You've been a little bit short with us since the power went out."

"Yeah, well…"

"Dean, it happens all the time up here. This is hardly something new and we're all doing fine with it. I think it was kind of fun having a picnic in front of the fire."

He threw the blanket he just took down onto the bed and turned to Abby. "You're right. It does happen all the time and normally it's just me here so it's not a big deal to be without power for a night, but it's not just me anymore! I have Maya to consider. I've been putting off getting a generator – and not for any good reason – and now we don't have heat or electricity and…and…she's just a kid! Kids need those things!"

Hearing his own words made Dean realize just how stressed he was and possibly how much he was overreacting. The look on Abby's face told him that she understood – again.

And even that pissed him off.

Why didn't she ever get upset or stressed out? How could she just keep going with the flow on everything? Didn't she realize how much he was screwing up? Didn't she care at all?

"Dean…"

"Did you see how scared she was when the lights went out?" he snapped. "If I had gotten the damn generator, she wouldn't have been."

"And did you just hear how she was a minute ago? She's fine, Dean. She's getting her pajamas on and she's excited about camping out in the living room. Everything's okay. There are going to be times when she gets scared or upset or just…things can't always be perfect and that's okay."

Realistically, he knew she was right, but it wasn't enough to make him feel any better.

"I hate that I wasn't prepared," he murmured.

Stepping in close to him, Abby cupped his face in her hands. "You did fine. We have the fire going for warmth, dinner was cooked, we have a small generator to keep the refrigerator going and we're going to have some cookies for dessert while we camp out and sleep in the living room. If anything, it's been a fun little adventure for her."

His response was a low, mirthless laugh.

"Let's get those pillows and blankets and everything all set up and then I'm going to change into my pajamas too," she said sweetly, kissing him on the cheek.

Just as she was about to move away from him, he wrapped his arms around her waist and held her close. "You still need a shirt?"

She nodded. "Please."

It would have been so easy to just kiss her and touch her and just…push the rest of the world away if only for a minute, but now wasn't the time. So he forced himself to move, grab a t-shirt out of his dresser drawer and scoop up the pillows and blankets. Together they went back out to the living room. Maya was already out there claiming her spot.

On the couch.

"Hey!" Abby said lightly, putting her hands on her hips. "How come you get the couch and we get the floor?"

"Because I was faster!" the little girl giggled. Then she jumped up and quickly scooted into the sleeping bag. "It's almost like sleeping in my bed!"

It was on the tip of Dean's tongue to reprimand her and remind her that Abby was their guest so she should get the couch, but then he realized that this way, he and Abby would be on the floor.

Together.

It wasn't ideal but…beggars couldn't be choosers.

\*\*\*\*

"Forget what I said earlier. This is great," Dean whispered against her ear later that night. Maya had been asleep for almost two hours and they were just getting settled under the blankets. Abby knew she shouldn't be enjoying it quite so much – and that they should have made up separate spaces to sleep, but because of the way the living room furniture was placed, they had a limited area to be near the fire. "Are you warm enough?"

She nodded and settled closer to him – her back to his front. Her bottom fit snugly against him and she cursed the fact that they weren't alone. "This is nice," she said softly. "The fire gives off a lot of heat and then we've got this whole body heat situation going on so I'm good."

"It could be better," he said, kissing her throat and nipping at her shoulder. "Although, you do look incredibly sexy in my shirt."

It was more like a dress on her and for a while she had worn it with a pair of leggings and socks. She was the kind of girl who hated to sleep with anything on her legs or feet, so she stripped them off once they got under the blankets.

"And I know you look even sexier out of it," he added.

"Behave yourself," she giggled. "There's a sleeping child less than five feet away."

"We could go inside for a little while. She'd never even know we were gone."

It was tempting.

Beyond tempting – especially with the way his lips were moving over her skin and his hands were starting to roam over her body. Stretching against him, Abby felt the full length of him behind her. He had on flannel pajama pants and no shirt and…well…she was only human. Dean had an amazing body and she enjoyed seeing it and touching it just as much as he seemed to enjoy doing the same to her.

What harm could an hour do?

*No!* She instantly admonished herself. They were adults and they had self-control, right?

Rolling over to face him, Abby kissed Dean's jaw. "You have no idea how much I want to take you up on that offer, but…"

He silenced her with a kiss – one of those that was hot and wet and deep and a little dirty but held so many promises. Sighing, she rolled onto her back as Dean stretched out on top of her taking the kiss even deeper.

It went on and on and on – her legs wrapped around his waist and his hands started to skim up her rib cage under her shirt and…

He stopped.

"Dammit," he murmured breathlessly. "I can't believe I'm going to say this but…"

"I know," she whispered, equally trying to catch her breath. "We need to stay out here."

Dean moved off of her and they shifted around until she was curled up against his side with his arm around her. "Being a responsible adult is hard."

Unable to help herself, she laughed softly.

"What's so…oh. I get it. Ha-ha," Dean teased.

"Sorry. My mind immediately went to the gutter on that one."

He hugged her close. "And I wouldn't want you any other way."

They stayed like that for several minutes and to Abby, it was so good, so perfect. Outside was quiet and peaceful as the snow continued to fall and inside other than the occasional pop from the fireplace, it was equally quiet.

"How are things going with the potential new dance studio?" he asked a few minutes later. "Any updates from Millie yet?"

"She mentioned something about a location over on White Street. I don't ever go over that way so I wasn't aware of it, but she texted me some pictures and said that she was going to talk to the owner to see what kind of money he was looking for and if it can be…you know…if we can turn the space into something we can use."

"What did you think from the pictures?"

Shrugging, Abby thought about how she wasn't overly impressed. In her mind, she pictured what she wanted and maybe she was being a little unrealistic with her expectations, but what was wrong with wanting what she wanted? And after looking at a few other places, she was beginning to lose hope, which is what she told Dean.

"If it doesn't work, it doesn't work," he said. "And I get where Millie's coming from – anything would be better than the one room at the community center. But it would be nice if you could make the move only once and have it be something you can make yours."

"Exactly," she said and then yawned. "I know this place would allow us to have four classrooms, but there's no stage and the rooms are a little small. Ideally I would like to have rooms where I can have space for at least twelve but up to twenty-four students."

"Do you think there's a need for that much?"

She nodded. "I've been asking around for a while and I get approached a lot by parents of older kids about classes. Then I'd like to offer classes for adults too. The possibilities are endless and…" She trailed off. She was a dreamer and she was getting a little bit ahead of herself. Maybe she should text Millie and tell her to make an offer and that the building would be okay. And then someday – hopefully – she'd be able to move some place bigger and better.

"And…?" Dean prompted.

"And…I don't know. It's just a dream, right? I mean, what are the odds that I'm going to find a place here in Silver Bell Falls that I can afford, that can be transformed into the exact kind of space that I need and that I'm going to be able to fill all those classes and make it my full-time job so I can quit the diner?"

"You don't like the diner?"

"It's certainly not my dream job."

He kissed her on the forehead. "I think it's great to have a dream and I also think that it's important to pursue it. There's a space out there for you, Abby. I'm sure of it. And when you find it, you will fill those classes because everyone in town loves you."

That didn't make her feel a whole lot better. "I don't want people taking classes because they feel obligated to. I want them to sign up because they want to learn how to dance."

"Still think it's going to happen," he said and then yawned. "I can't believe it's only ten o'clock and I'm half asleep."

"Mmm…me too," she said sleepily. "But I think it's because I'm so comfortable like this." Under the blankets, her legs tangled with Dean's until they were both comfortable. "Hopefully the power will be back on in the morning and the snow will have stopped."

"I'm in no rush," he said quietly. "I like having you here with me." Dean's voice trailed off by the last word and Abby knew he was just about asleep.

She waited a few minutes to say, "And I really like being here with you."

****

As predicted, the snow had stopped the next morning, the power was back on and the roads were being cleared. By lunchtime, they were up and heading into town. Abby had tried to graciously bow out because she needed to get home and decorate her own tree, but Maya insisted that they should decorate both trees today together.

An ambitious tactic, but Dean was in full agreement.

Abby seemed a little less certain.

Dean had to convince her that they could get it all done and, in the end, she agreed. It just meant that they were going to have to shop a lot quicker than usual.

No easy task with a five-year old who was easily distracted.

"Remember what we talked about," he whispered to Maya when he helped her out of the car at the mall. "We have two Christmas trees at two different houses to get decorated today and we don't have a lot of time."

"I know, I know," she huffed. "And it's a school night and I can't look at toys and I can't get ice cream…"

He hugged her close before putting her down. "Good girl."

As usual, his niece surprised him by going into the first store and instantly finding the ornaments that she wanted – two Disney princess ones, a snowman, and a box of pink satin Christmas balls with silver glitter designs. All in all, she was quick and efficient. They were heading up to the register to pay when she stopped.

"You okay, Maya?" he asked. Dean looked and saw that she stopped in front of a display of tree toppers. He walked over to her and crouched down. "See one you like?"

She never took her eyes off of the display. "Do you have something for the top of your tree?" she asked quietly.

"I have a star."

"Oh."

"But if you see something here that you'd rather have, we can do that."

Wordlessly, she reached for an angel and handed it to Dean.

He was confused. Maya was excited about all of the other decorations she'd found. Why was this tree topper making her sad?

Before she could move away, he reached for her hand and waited for her to look at him.

"She looks like my mom. And my mom's an angel now."

*Gutted.*

That was exactly how he felt. Abby was standing next to him and he handed her the angel, then picked up Maya and held her close. He knew he was fighting back tears but he felt hers trailing down his neck as she silently wept.

He had no idea how long they stood there like that, but when Maya lifted her head, he wiped away her tears. Looking around, he spotted Abby by the register paying for their decorations. She was talking to Ramona the cashier and smiling. When he walked over, he heard the tail end of the conversation.

"…it's a great location and I know my aunt's been dying to see someone come in and take it over," Ramona was saying. "You should look into it."

"I will and I appreciate the information. Thanks, Ramona!" With a smile and a wave, Abby joined them. She took his hand and together they walked back out to the car.

They had decided to decorate Abby's tree first – mainly because of the time and Dean knew that it would be easier to get Maya to bed on time if they ended the day at their house. Abby didn't mind.

The ride was short and spent in virtual silence, which Dean figured was for the best. Maya needed the time and honestly, so did he. Decorating Abby's tree was the perfect distraction and – as usual – she seemed to know that because as soon as they stepped into her house, she put them each to work on a different task.

Dean strung the lights while Abby had Maya help her carefully unwrap some of the ornaments and get them organized. They made hot chocolate while they waited for him to finish with the lights – apparently Abby liked a lot of them on her tree – and then they came out and hung Abby's stockings on her mantle.

"How come you have two stockings?" Maya asked.

"One is for me and one is for my mom. She's going to come and visit for Christmas."

Maya nodded, her face solemn. "My mom can't come and visit."

Damn. So much for the distraction. He was about to say something but Abby was already ahead of him.

"You know, I bet your mom is watching you from heaven right now," she began. "And I'm sure it makes her happy that you and your uncle have each other and that you're going to spend Christmas together."

Maya nodded again. "I miss her."

"Oh, sweetie," Abby said, pulling Maya in for a hug. "She misses you too."

Dean finished with the lights and walked over to sit with the two of them, hugging them both. This was supposed to be fun – something happy for them to do – and he had no idea how to turn it around.

"Tell you what," Abby said after a moment, "let's get my tree decorated so we can get to your house and you can put your new angel on the top of your tree. That way, your mom will be there with you. What do you say?"

A small smile crossed Maya's face. "Okay." Then she stood up and hugged Abby one more time. "Thank you, Abby."

"You're welcome, sweetheart."

"I love you," the little girl said and Dean actually heard Abby stop breathing for a moment.

"I love you too," Abby said softly, squeezing Maya. When they finally broke apart, Abby began directing her on which ornaments to start hanging on the tree. Maya went right to work but before Abby could move away, Dean stood and made her look at him.

"You okay?"

She nodded. "I guess…I don't know…I wasn't expecting that."

"Me either."

"You're not upset, are you?"

"About her missing Karen?"

"Well that and…you know…what she said to me."

"I didn't think about how certain situations would make her feel or what would trigger her to suddenly remember that she misses Karen. One minute she's fine and then the next…she's just sad. My parents mentioned that I should look into counseling for her but…part of me hoped that she wouldn't need it. Maybe she does."

"It might be a good thing for her."

He nodded. "And as for what she said to you…" Pausing, he let his gaze hold hers for a moment and he swore he could almost see the answer to everything right there in her emerald eyes. "I'm glad that she feels that way about you."

"You…you are?"

Nodding again, he replied, "I am."

"Oh," she sighed. "Good."

"Do you know why?"

Abby shook her head.

"Because that's how I feel about you too." His voice was low and soft, so that only she could hear him. "I'm in love with you, Abby."

Her eyes went wide.

Reaching up, Dean caressed her cheek and rested his forehead against hers. "I probably should have found a better time or way to tell you, but…it's true."

"Oh, Dean…"

"Don't say anything. Not now." He looked toward the tree and then back at her. "Let's decorate and just…we'll talk about this more later. I just really wanted you to know how I felt." Then he chuckled softly. "I kind of wish Maya hadn't said it first."

Abby laughed with him and then kissed him. Lifting her head, she smiled. "I think it was all perfect."

"Okay," he said, relaxing. "Let's get to work."

Abby nodded but when Dean went to move away, she reached for his hand. "Oh, and Dean?"

"Yeah?"

She leaned in close again. "I love you too."

\*\*\*\*

They stood back and looked at their handiwork.

"Well, what do you think?" Abby asked. They had finished her tree hours ago and now they had just placed the angel at the top of Dean and Maya's tree. Before anyone answered, she walked over and shut off the overhead light so that only the tree illuminated the room.

"Ooh…" Maya said with awe. "It's the most beautiful tree ever."

Dean picked her up and held her close. "I think we did a great job on our first tree, kiddo. I know this is the best tree I've ever had."

"Really?"

He nodded. "Yup. All of your ornaments were exactly what my tree has been missing all these years."

Abby stood back, unsure if she should say anything or let them have this moment.

She opted to let them have the moment.

Quietly she walked to the kitchen and cleared away the last of the dishes from their dinner earlier. On the ride from her house to theirs, they stopped and grabbed burgers to bring home to eat. There wasn't much to do but she wanted to give the two of them a few minutes to themselves without her hovering.

Plus, it was the first time she had been alone or had time to think about what Dean said to her earlier.

He loved her.

She certainly hadn't been prepared for that, hadn't seen it coming. Well…she had hoped but…and she knew Dean cared for her, but to be in love with her? It was still hard to wrap her brain around it. It was wonderful and exciting and terrifying all at once.

Abby knew her feelings for him were real. She'd been dealing with them for a long time, but Dean's life was in such a state of chaos right now that she was having a hard time believing that he could possibly feel this way about her. Maybe he was confused. Maybe he thought it was how he felt because of all they were sharing. Or maybe…

"Here you are," Dean said as he walked into the kitchen. "We were wondering where you went."

"I thought it would be nice for the two of you to have a moment with your newly-decorated tree. It turned out beautiful."

He nodded. "It did and Maya's thrilled. She's going to put on her pajamas and asked if she could have some cookies in front of the tree before bed."

Abby chuckled. "She probably shouldn't have cookies right before bed, but I guess it's a special occasion so…"

"That's what I thought." Walking over to her, Dean instantly wrapped his arms around her waist and pulled her close. "Hi."

She smiled. "Hi."

"Thanks for coming with us today."

"My pleasure. It was a lot of fun and I have to admit, this is the first time I got to decorate two trees. I kind of liked it."

He laughed softly. "It was a first for me as well. But I'm kind of hoping it will be a last too."

Confused, Abby only looked at him.

"I was hoping that next year there would only be one tree. Our tree."

Her heart kicked a hard beat at his words. "Oh…" she sighed, smiling. "That does sound nice."

"Maybe I'm getting a little ahead of myself but…"

Footsteps running down the hall stopped his words.

"Can you stay after Maya goes to bed?"

There were so many things Abby needed to get done at home. With the snowstorm and the trees and spending the night the previous night, the last thing she should say was yes, but…

"Sure, but not too late. I really haven't been home all weekend and I have to hit the ground running tomorrow. The extra practices for the Christmas recital and the parade start so…"

"Okay. I promise not to keep you too late," he said with a sheepish grin. "Even though I'd really like to keep you here all night."

That was exactly what she was thinking but…

He kissed her before she could say anything more.

# Eleven

Ten days.

Ten long, exhausting days.

Dean thought working from home was going to work to his advantage, but it didn't. He was busier than usual with new projects and proposals coming in and his workday was technically shortened on the days he picked up Maya after school.

When Abby said she had to hit the ground running and that the extra practices would keep her busy, she wasn't kidding. They saw each other on the days that Maya had ballet and he had managed to persuade her to have dinner with them twice, but she was distracted by the things she needed to be doing.

Costume fittings, stage props and designs, parade meetings, photo sessions with her classes, and what seemed like an endless search for new studio space. All of a sudden it seemed as if there were nothing but vacant buildings in Silver Bell Falls. And now that the town knew she was looking, everyone was approaching her with suggestions and big plans to have her in her own space by the beginning of the new year.

Dean knew it was a temporary thing – this all had to do with the Christmas season – but he couldn't help but be disappointed by their lack of time together.

The last time they'd spent any quality time together was the day they decorated their trees. She'd stayed after Maya went to bed and they talked late into the night – effectively making him break his promise to her – but Abby hadn't seemed to mind. If anything, she'd been happy – like him. They'd laughed and talked and…Dean couldn't help but feel like it was just a small glimpse into the life they could have together.

If they could just get through Christmas!

Maya had ballet today so he knew he'd get to see Abby and he also knew that Maya's class was her last class of the day. With any luck, he'd be able to persuade her to go to dinner with them. She'd insist on the diner because it was close and he'd agree because some time with her was better than none at all. Dean found himself longing for the day when they could all go home together.

Pulling up to the community center, he parked and just sat there for a moment – trying to wrap his brain around all of it.

He was ready for their future together to start now.

If anything, the sooner the better.

His and Maya's lives were already in a state of transition and being with Abby made it easier. Wouldn't it be great if they could all just…transition together? It was so easy to see them being a family and living together in his home – for now – and then after the first of the year they could find someplace bigger so they could possibly even grow as a family.

Children of his own.

His heart did a little squeeze at the thought.

For so long Dean knew he wanted a family, but didn't have anyone special to make him want to take that step.

Abby made him want to take that step.

It was crazy that now that he was thinking of it, he was excited at the possibilities and with that excitement came a touch of impatience. Now that he knew exactly what he wanted for the rest of his life, he wanted it to begin right now!

With his mind reeling, he remembered that Abby's mother was coming in for Christmas. What if they could get married at Christmas? Neither of them had large families and while he knew his parents would want to be there, he wasn't sure they'd come on such short notice and deal with the cold.

Maybe they could have a New Year's Eve wedding! He thought. How festive that would be! There was always a big celebration in Silver Bell and he knew he could get the whole town involved to help them out!

It was perfect!

It would be romantic and wonderful and...

A loud banging on his car window nearly scared him to death.

Josiah.

Climbing from the car, he let out a low laugh. "Dude, you scared the hell out of me."

Josiah laughed with him. "You were just sitting in there and I've been trying to get your attention for a few minutes. You okay?"

Smiling from ear to ear, he replied, "Yeah. I am. I really am."

He noticed the surprise on his friend's face and decided to share with him what he'd just thought of in his car.

"So…wait. You want to marry Abby? Like…for real?"

"What do you mean for real?"

"As in you're in love with her and not just wanting to get married for the sake of convenience?"

The wave of anger that hit him was unexpected. His smile faded as he faced Josiah. "What the hell is that supposed to mean? Why would I marry Abby for convenience?"

Josiah took a tentative step back. "I'm just saying that it all seems a little…coincidental. You barely knew Abby before Maya came to live with you and then she starts helping you out and then you're dating and now you want to marry her. Dean, seriously, you need to think about this and not rush into it."

"I'm not rushing this, I…"

"Dude, you're rushing it. It's been just a little over a month…"

"How fast did you fall in love with Melanie?" Dean interrupted.

Frowning, Josiah glared at him for a moment. "Not the same thing."

"It's exactly the same thing. Three weeks. You fell in love with her in three weeks. You were living together after two. How is this any different?"

"Because it's you, dammit!" Josiah snapped. "Dean, you're my best friend and I know you better than you think. You've been living a solitary life for so damn long and now you're going from one extreme to the other." He paused and sighed. "Look, I'm not saying that you don't love Abby – if you say you do, then you do, but that doesn't mean you have to marry her right now."

"You have no idea," Dean began, his voice so low it was a near growl. "My whole life I've had to put how I feel and what I want aside because I had to be cautious. I have missed out on so much because I was too scared to take a chance and actually live! Well now I want to live! I want to be happy and I want Maya to be happy and I want Abby to be happy! And you know what? I think we can all have that if we can be together as a family!"

"Okay, but…"

"No!" Dean instantly interrupted. "It's not the same as what you and Melanie had. It was just the two of you. I have Maya to consider and Abby and I know that we can't just live together. That's not the right example to set and I certainly don't want to give the town anything to gossip about."

"You're letting the past play too much into this," Josiah countered. "No one thinks about comparing you to your sister anymore – they haven't in a long time. You need to move on from that. People live together all the time."

Dean shook his head. "I won't do that to Maya. Her life was turned upside down already. She lost both of her parents and her life hasn't been the least bit stable. I'm trying to change that. I *need* to change that for her. When Abby and I get married…"

"Have you even talked to Abby about any of this?"

"What…about getting married?"

Josiah nodded.

"Not exactly. Not yet. But…that's the direction we're heading in. I know it and if we could just get some time alone so we could talk about it, I know she'd agree with me. It makes perfect sense. Why should we wait?"

"I can't argue with you on the waiting part because it's exactly how I felt with Melanie, but…here we are a year later and we're not married and we're okay."

"But you're living together," Dean argued. "For all intents and purposes, you're married. You're just missing the piece of paper. And again, it's not the same for us. We have…"

"I get it. You have Maya. But don't you think it would be just as devastating for her if you rushed into this marriage too soon and then you and Abby end up divorcing?"

Dean opened his mouth to say something and then instantly closed it.

He hadn't thought of that.

In his mind, he and Abby were forever. He knew it. He could feel it. But what if Josiah was right? What if…?

"Look, I can't tell you how you feel or how Abby feels, and there are plenty of people who get married after knowing each other for shorter periods of time than the two of you. I just want you to be careful and really think on this before you just jump in. No matter what you decide, I'm going to be right there with you supporting you. You know that, right?"

And he did. It takes a real friend to point out when you might be making a mistake and yet still promise to be there for you.

Nodding, Dean replied, "I do. And…thanks."

"No one deserves to be happy more than you and I think Abby is great. I care about you both and don't want to see either of you get hurt."

It would be easy to say that they weren't going to get hurt, but who was he kidding? He had no control over that.

But he couldn't wait to prove his friend wrong.

\*\*\*\*

"…and then I'm supposed to go over to Silver Street and look at some property!" Abby said with a bit of a huff as she walked around the classroom and picked up trash that had been left behind. "Why can't people throw out their paper and water bottles?"

"What time do you need to go look at the property?"

Looking over at the clock on the wall, she sighed and seemed to pick up her pace. "In fifteen minutes." She threw the trash out and quickly walked over to the corner where she kept her gym bag and pulled out a sweatshirt. "I'm really hoping this is going to be the place. On paper it seems like it will work for almost everything we need. The price is something I can definitely afford – with the investors – and if we can agree on everything, I can take occupancy on it by January 2."

"Abby! That's great!" Dean walked over and scooped her up in his arms and spun her around before kissing her. "Are you excited?"

She smiled but it felt a little forced. "I am. I really am. I think." She paused. "It's just a bit much right now. I swear I'm already barely holding on by a thread with all I have to do and this is just one more thing on my plate." Putting the sweatshirt on, she pulled out her scarf and quickly wrapped that around her too.

"Then I've got my mom coming in and the recital and the parade and there's been some issues with the costumes…" Another pause. "I normally take the first week of January to simply sit and do nothing because I'm physically ill from pushing myself too much and it looks like I won't even get to do that this year. I'll still be sick, but I'll have to work through it. Fun times."

Fluttering around the room, Abby saw that everything was in its place and then smiled distractedly at Dean. "I'm sorry, but I really need to get going." Then she looked around again. "Where's Maya?"

"Out in the lobby talking to Jenny," he said and she could tell something was bothering him.

"Are you okay? Is everything all right? Maya didn't mention anything when I picked her up…"

He shook his head and gave her a half-hearted smile. "I was hoping we could have dinner tonight, but I know you're busy and you have a lot going on. I just miss you."

Her shoulders sagged as she looked at him. "I miss you too. I both love and hate this time of year. I long for the day when I have a studio of my own and more people working with me so that it's not all on my shoulders." Stepping in close, she kissed him.

"What can I do to help you?" he asked and the sincerity in his voice almost made her cry. It wasn't often that anyone asked her that and she wasn't sure how to handle it.

But she found a way.

"Tell you what, why don't you go and get Maya and I'll meet you both at the diner in about forty-five minutes? Will that work?"

"Are you sure? You just said…"

Abby placed a finger over his lips to silence him. "I know and you reminded me that I also need to take some time for myself. I really didn't want to go home and cook and Dan made his famous meatloaf at the diner today. A little comfort food on a cold night sounds perfect."

He pulled her in close and kissed her again. "You're perfect."

Chuckling, Abby moved out of his embrace. "Hardly, but I'm glad you think so." Another glance at the clock showed she was going to be late. "I really need to run. See you at the diner!"

She waved to Kathy and Jenny and Maya as she ran out the door. The drive over to Silver Street took all of three minutes and yet it was so filled with anxiety that made it feel much longer. This was the place. Deep in her heart Abby knew it and yet she was afraid to get her hopes up.

Millie was waiting out front along with her realtor, Bette, and Alima Levy who owned the building. They were all talking and smiling and looked…professional and prepared. Abby looked down at herself and groaned. Why hadn't she thought to change out of her leggings and sweatshirt?

"Too late now," she murmured, grabbing her purse and climbing from the car. With a smile plastered on her face, she approached the trio of women and greeted them.

"Abby," Millie said with a huge smile, "I think this is it. It has the most square footage and it's already got walls up to give you four classrooms and there's a large storage area in the back that can be transformed into a stage and practice area!"

Abby nodded and was about to comment when Bette chimed in. "Let's get out of the cold and go in and take a look." They followed her to the door and Abby's heart beat wildly in her chest. Both Bette and Alima were talking about all of the features of the building and Abby knew it was for her benefit, but once she walked through the door, she didn't need words.

She was envisioning it all.

Four rooms that, with a little bit of work, could be easily transformed into studio spaces for classes.

The large entryway could be transformed into a reception area with the addition of a desk and if she added some comfortable chairs, it would work beautifully as a waiting area.

And the storage area was a wonderful blank slate that would probably take the most work but in Abby's mind, she could already see the stage set up and part of the room serving as a storage area for props and costumes and dressing rooms.

"It is zoned for commercial use," Bette said as Abby continued to wander around. "The whole town is on board with this project, Abby, so I don't think you'll have any problems moving forward."

"With a little elbow grease from a team of volunteers," Millie chimed in, "we can have this place painted and cleaned up in no time."

Finally Alima weighed in. "For a long time now, I had no idea what to do with this space. Now I know it was waiting for this project." She paused. "So what do you think, Abby? Will it work?"

"I…I'm having a hard time figuring out how I'll get it all done," Abby began cautiously, a tremble in her voice. Her emotions were running high – she wanted this to work and knew that it could – but she was overwhelmed by looking around at all of the work that needed to be done.

"For starters, I've already got committees ready and waiting," Millie said, grinning.

"Committees?"

"Let's see, we have a cleaning committee for starters. The ladies from Four Friends cleaning have volunteered to come in and help – Lynn, Patricia, Chris and Helena. I know they'll do a great job but I called on another group to come in and help and they're all dance moms – Rhonda, Chrissy, Pam and Carol – their daughters are all in your intermediate ballet class."

If she thought she was overwhelmed before, she was seriously mistaken. How had everyone known about this and not mentioned it to her? She asked Millie just that.

"Well, I told everyone to keep it quiet until we found a place. I'm a planner and I just really wanted to get things in place so we were ready to go as soon as you gave the word."

"I think I'm a little in shock," Abby said with a nervous chuckle. "How…I mean…what else have you set up?"

"Shawn at the paint store said she and her husband are willing to donate the paint supplies – rollers, brushes, drop cloths, that sort of thing. And Stracey has some artwork over at the boutique that she wants to donate for the walls, Bev is organizing food to feed everyone while the work is going on and Jennifer and Monique at the antique shop have some beautiful chairs they're going to donate for the lobby."

"Oh my…"

Bette stepped forward and smiled. "I was talking with Kathy Jones and she said she has found you several candidates to work the front desk so you can focus on teaching the classes and not have to worry about answering phones and dealing with people coming in and out with questions."

"Already?" Abby asked, still shocked at all of this information.

Bette nodded. "Last I heard there were three ladies – Kim, Eileen and Shannon – I'm terrible with last names – who were very excited about the possibility of volunteering their time."

"Volunteering? But…I can't ask people to do that. I need to fill the classes and figure out a budget and then I can see about hiring people and…"

Millie held up a hand to stop her. "Christine Miles – you know her, she's an accountant, has her office over on Main by the diner? Well, she is offering one year of her services to help you get started."

Tears swam in Abby's eyes. Could this all really be happening? Could it really be this easy?

"I have a team of contractors that I use on all of my properties," Alima said. "Bette can vouch for them that they do great work. They're each willing to donate two days of their time to coming in and doing whatever you need – carpentry, plumbing, electric – all of it. This place is structurally sound and I have the inspection certificates for you, but I'm sure there are some special things you're going to want to do. So all you need to do is work up your plans and let the guys see them and they'll help you get it done."

"Carol Owens over at the hardware store mentioned that she could get you a really good deal on the mirrors for the dance rooms," Millie said.

"And Pam over at the copy place said she'd help out with flyers and business cards – five hundred of each – to help you get started.," Alima said.

Now her tears freely fell. "Is the whole town involved?"

The three women nodded.

"Pretty much," Millie said, her own eyes going misty. "I told you I was going to make it happen, Abby. As soon as I said what we were looking to do, my phone hasn't stopped ringing!" She stepped forward, placing her hands on Abby's shoulders. "You are a treasure to the people of Silver Bell Falls. You give so much of yourself to your students and to the town and this is our way of saying thank you."

"I am simply blown away," Abby said, her voice thick with emotion. "I never expected…this is more than I ever thought…"

"Is this a yes?" Millie asked excitedly. "Is this the future home of Silver Bell Falls Dance Studio?" Then she laughed. "Or whatever you'd like to name it?"

They all laughed and Abby wiped away some of her tears. "I…I think it is!"

"Oh my goodness! That's great!" Millie cried.

"I've got papers all set for you!" Bette said, smiling.

"And I'm thrilled that you're going to be the new owner of this place," Alima added.

"Oh my God," Abby said suddenly. "Owner. I'm going to be an owner." Her heart was almost beating right out of her chest as panic set in. "What if I can't get approval from the bank? What if I can't afford this place? What if...?"

"Gwenn at the bank is expecting you tomorrow and has every confidence that you'll be approved," Millie said, handing Abby a card.

"I've negotiated a fabulous deal for you," Bette added and then smiled at Alima. "We all really believe in this project and we know you're going to do amazing things here."

"Fab...what kind of deal? This place is the biggest we've seen and I know what the prices were on those other places." Abby looked at Alima. "I want this to be a fair deal for you. Please don't expect me to be okay with you losing money on this deal."

Alima smiled and shook her head. "Abby, this place has been empty for a long time. I've been doing maintenance on it and taking care of it but you are doing me a favor by taking it and loving it and making it a wonderful place again." Then she stepped in a little closer. "Besides, I heard a rumor about some Zumba classes! My girlfriends and I are very excited at the possibility – especially after the holidays!"

They all laughed again.

"I mentioned that to my friends Isha and Laura," Bette said, "and we're looking forward to that too!"

"Oh my…it looks like I'm definitely going to have at least one full class!" Abby said happily. "I…I don't know what to say!"

"Say that you've found your place and that you're looking forward to starting to work on it after the first of the year," Millie said.

Nodding furiously, Abby agreed. "I can't believe it! I have a dance studio!" And all she could think of was how she couldn't wait to share the news with Dean. "So…what's next?"

"I know it's late so let's plan on meeting at my office in the morning to sign the papers and then you can head over to the bank before going in to work at the diner," Bette suggested. "Will that work for you?"

Abby laughed. "Are you kidding me? I'll make it work!"

"How about we say eight tomorrow morning?" Bette asked, taking out her calendar.

"I'll be there!"

Walking out the door, Abby felt like she was floating on air. Actually, what she really wanted to do was have a few minutes alone in the space to simply dance and get out all of her excitement and energy and celebrate, but that would have to wait. There was no way she was going to ask for a key before they even signed any contracts.

No matter how much she wanted to.

"Do you want to go and grab a drink to celebrate?" Millie asked as Bette locked the door.

"Thanks, but I'm meeting Dean and Maya for dinner," Abby said and saw the knowing smile on all three women's faces. "What? What did I say?"

"I just think that it's wonderful that you're dating Dean Hayes," Bette said as she put her keys away. "It's been nice to see him out and about with you these last couple of weeks. And what a blessing you are to his niece."

"Oh…um…"

"I agree," Alima said as they started to walk away from the building. "I'm sure the two of them would be lost without you. Such a sad situation. Dean's lucky to have you."

"Uh…"

"I think the three of you just make the sweetest looking little family," Millie added and then let out a light giggle. "That's exactly what I think whenever I see you together. I'm so happy for all of you."

"Dean and I are just dating," Abby said, feeling the need to clarify things. No need for people to start gossiping and speculating. It was one thing for her to be wishing for more or seeing more to their relationship than maybe there was, but the last thing she needed was for people to start talking like this to Dean. They'd probably scare him off!

"Oh…well, I just thought…" Millie began, "it seemed like…"

Abby waved her off. "It's okay. Really. But I need to get going to meet them! Have a good night!" Thanking Millie, Bette and Alima one more time, she ran to her car and then sat and let everything that just happened sink in.

Her own studio.

Her own business.

In Silver Bell Falls.

It was a dream come true.

And while she was thrilled and excited and practically bouncing in her seat, the practical side of her began to kick in and reminded her of everything she was going to have to do over the next few weeks and how – like she had mentioned to Dean earlier – she wasn't going to get a break after New Year's. It was going to be like stepping from one form of chaos into another.

*Yes, but it's chaos for the greater good!* She reminded herself.

Teaching the classes and prepping for all of the holiday festivities was great for her students and the town. It all always left her feeling good, but there was a bit of a letdown at the end of each holiday season when it was just her sitting by herself. She knew how happy the performances made the residents of her beloved town, but…at the end of the day, she was celebrating alone.

*Not anymore.*

True, now she had Dean and Maya to share all of this with, and her mom too, but…with so much on her plate, how much time was she really going to be able to spend with them over the next couple of months? The holidays, the renovations and then getting the studio started and then…

"My head hurts from all of this," she murmured, resting her head on the back of her seat. When she started her car, she saw it was almost time to meet Dean and Maya at the diner, but she had a few extra minutes and decided to call her mom and tell her the news.

Then she'd go and celebrate with her two favorite Silver Bell residents and hope that they would understand when she explained that their already-limited time together was about to get even more limited.

But it wasn't forever and it was for a good cause.

Dean would understand, right?

# Twelve

After dinner, they walked out to their cars together and Dean helped Maya into her booster seat before turning to Abby. "So this is all great news, right?"

She was smiling and nodding and talking about all of her plans but Dean was having a hard time feeling excited for her. He saw the happiness on her face and heard the enthusiasm in her voice and yet it all meant one thing – less time together.

It was selfishness, pure and simple and yet…he couldn't help it.

Here he was ready to pour out his heart and ask her to plan her future with him but she was suddenly busy making plans for a future without him.

*Okay, dramatic much*? He chided himself.

It wasn't like she was cutting him out of her life, but it kind of felt that way. In all of her talk about the plans for the next several months, he wasn't mentioned once. She wasn't asking him for any help or any input. Abby simply had a plan in place that didn't include him.

And that stung.

A lot.

Word had spread around Silver Bell pretty fast because all through dinner, people came over to the table to congratulate her and tell her how they were planning on volunteering to help her get the new dance studio ready for spring classes. And through it all Dean had smiled and said how happy he was and Maya had chimed in to talk about how excited she was for a new dance studio.

And he felt like a traitor.

Why now?

Why did everything have to change right now?

"What do you say to pizza and Netflix Friday night?" he asked, hoping that he didn't come off sounding as annoyed as he thought he did.

Abby looked at him oddly. "Dean, I was just telling you about how I'm going to be working with the festival committee on props for the recital on Friday night." She chuckled. "Sorry." Then she kissed him on the cheek. "I know I've been talking a lot tonight. I'm just…*gah*! I just can't believe this is all really happening! I know earlier I was all freaked out about how much I have to do and how it was killing me, but now? I'm kind of jazzed up about it! My mind is just racing and racing and racing and…ooh! I should probably see about calling my girlfriend Jacqueline. She used to study jazz. She lives in Albany now but maybe she'd consider coming and teaching here."

Pulling out her phone, Dean watched as she began to furiously type out a text message and he sighed. "Abby…?"

"I really should go. I feel like I have a million phone calls to make and it's already getting late." She looked up at him and smiled. "I'll see you Friday for Maya's class."

When she turned to walk away, something in him snapped.

"So that's it?" he asked loudly.

"What do you…?"

"Abby, I get that you're excited and that you have a lot to do but…what's going on here? With us?"

He almost cringed at how needy he sounded.

"What are you talking about?"

Sighing with frustration, he raked a hand through his hair and stared at her. "I have listened to you talk for the last ninety minutes about all that you have planned for the next several months and you know what you left out?"

Brow furrowed, he could tell that she was trying to figure it out and that just served to tick him off more.

"Me! Maya! You have all these plans, Abby, and not once did you mention spending time with us!"

Abby's eyes went wide at his words.

"How do you think that makes me feel?" he asked, his own voice gruff with emotion.

"Dean, I…I don't even know what to say to that," she said and she sounded more than a little bit cautious.

Taking a steadying breath, he did his best to calm down. The car door was open and although they were standing several feet away, he didn't want Maya to hear the conversation. "Look, I really am happy for you because I know this whole studio thing is what you've been wanting – what you've been working toward. But what about us? I feel like we've gotten into a good place together and that you're just putting us aside."

"I guess…I mean I didn't think it would be a big deal. In my mind, I saw this as part of my job and that you'd understand that. If your job was going to keep you busy, I know I would understand. I might not like it and I'd miss you and our time together but I'd never make you choose."

Was that what he was really asking? He wondered.

Unfortunately, he knew the answer.

He was.

"It's not just me, Abby. There's Maya and she looks forward to her time with you and seeing you after school and…"

"Is that what this is about?" she asked, irritation clearly lacing her tone. "Are you worried because I won't be as readily available to help you with Maya after school? Because if we are, then you should remember that from the very beginning, I said I would help until you got things worked out. I never said I could do it forever."

Okay, now they were getting somewhere and it wasn't good.

"That's not what I was getting at," he countered. "All I was saying was that it's not just me and you in this relationship. There are three of us and…"

"And I get that, Dean. I really do. But you're basically telling me that I can either have my dream job or you and Maya! How is that fair?"

"It's not…"

"But it is," she said flatly. "You know, when I was done touring the building tonight, I couldn't wait to come and share the news with you. I couldn't wait to bring you over and show it to you and walk around the place and tell you my ideas." Taking a step back, she quickly swiped at her eyes and Dean suspected she was on the verge of crying. "I didn't expect this – the building, the town helping out so much, or you and Maya. I never expected any of it."

"Abby," he said softly, but as he took a step toward her, she took a step back. "I didn't expect any of this either." And then he decided to lay it all out on the line. "But now that I found you and I see the direction my life is taking, I'm excited about it. I think of the future – our future – and it's like I can't wait for it to start!"

"Dean…"

"I want to marry you and have a family with you," he said earnestly. "Don't you get that? For the first time in my life I'm actually ready to live my life and I want to live it with you!"

Tears flowed down Abby's cheeks faster than she could wipe them away. "I want all of that too," she said quietly. "I really do. You have no idea how happy it makes me to see you out and embracing life and how easily you've transitioned into the role of father to Maya."

And that's when it hit him.

There was going to be a "but."

"But…" he promoted, his throat felt raw even as he said it.

"But…" she began and then took a moment to seemingly collect her thoughts. "This is something I have to do right now. And it shouldn't be something that I have to choose between." Taking a step toward him, Abby reached for his hands but he held back. "We can have everything you mentioned, Dean. We can. It's just not going to happen right this minute. I mean…you weren't thinking of us getting married now were you?"

In for a penny…

"I was." Defiance echoed through his words as he held himself stiffly before her. "I wanted us to get married while your mother was here. I thought it would be the perfect time because you'd be done with the recitals and the parades and the holidays and…it made perfect sense."

A small smile crossed those beautiful lips, but it was a sad one. "Oh."

"Yeah…oh."

"You've obviously thought a lot about this."

He nodded.

"You gave yourself the time to think about it and figure it out and from where I'm standing, it all works out very well for you. The problem is…you never talked to me about this. You never took the time to let me figure things out." She shook her head and looked down at the ground before meeting his gaze again. "You didn't take the time to get to know me."

"I do know you, Abby, and that's why I fell in love with you. You're this amazing woman who brings laughter and light into everyone's lives, especially into my life. Before I met you, it was like I was a half of a person, living half of a life. When I'm with you, I feel whole – like I never have before in my life. And when I'm not with you, a part of me is missing."

"Do you hear what you're saying?" she asked, her voice barely a whisper. "It's all about how you feel and your life."

Her shoulders sagged as she took a small step back and that's when he knew.

He'd lost her.

"I can't do this right now, Dean," she said after a long moment. "I think…I think we need some time apart."

"Abby…"

But she shook her head to stop him. "It's kind of clear that we both have a lot to think about and I can't do that standing here with you in the middle of a parking lot." She wiped more tears away. "I…I gotta go."

And then she turned and walked away and possibly out of his life.

**** 

How it was possible to go through the twelve stages of grief during a twelve-minute drive, Abby wasn't sure. And yet…she'd done it.

Okay, not twelve, but at least five.

Dammit.

It wasn't until she was inside her house and taking off her coat that she was able to just let loose like she wanted – needed – to.

Blindsided. That was the only way she could fully describe how she felt. Collapsing on her sofa, she tried to recall any conversation she and Dean had ever had that could have prepared her for this, but there were none. While Abby knew where her feelings for him were going – were actually already there – she hadn't realized that Dean felt the same way.

Marriage? Already? The only time they talked about that was after Maya had made that comment to him and it was one time! When had he suddenly come to this decision? And what was his rush? Abby understood his reasoning to a point – he was finally excited about the future but…what he was suggesting wasn't practical!

Was it?

And asking her to choose between her dream job and him? How was that fair? They had been talking about this almost since the beginning of their relationship. Abby never tried to hide what she wanted or what she was trying to achieve – with Millie's help! So now that it was actually happening, why was he so against it?

So where did this leave her? What was she supposed to do and how was she supposed to choose or decide?

"I want them both," she sighed.

And that was it, really. That was her decision. She wanted Dean. She wanted Maya. And she wanted her studio.

Couldn't he see that the studio would be something for them to work on together? That it was going to be a place that Maya would benefit from? Hell, it was some place that Abby would benefit from because it was going to be hers and it made her happy! She'd be able to dance all day and share her love of it with so many others! Didn't her happiness play into his plans at all?

Sadness overwhelmed her.

Why should Dean be any different? It would seem that this was the pattern of her life. Abby was a giver.

She would do anything to help a friend and she never expected anything in return.

And that's usually what she got.

She'd been taken advantage of more than her fair share and as much as it pained her even to think about it, maybe that was Dean's deal all along and he was just doing his best to sugarcoat the situation.

Maybe he didn't really love her and all she'd been was a convenience to help him through a difficult time.

Tears burned her eyes but for the first time tonight, she didn't fight them or try to hold them back. She let them fall.

And they continued to fall for a very long time.

****

Abby walked around town like a zombie the next day.

Bette had attributed the dark circles under her eyes to staying up all night celebrating. Gwenn at the bank mistook Abby's quiet demeanor for nerves. When she arrived at the diner for work, though, Bev took one look at her and knew something was wrong.

"Okay, sit," she ordered once Abby came out of the back room.

Looking around the diner, Abby saw it was empty. "I've got stuff to do, Bev, and I was already five minutes late."

"Dan! Do you care that Abby was five minutes late?" she called out.

"Nope! Find out why she looks like someone just killed her dog!" Dan called out from the kitchen.

With a sigh, Abby sat at the counter and put her head down.

"That bad, huh?"

"You have no idea," Abby replied and then took a minute before sitting back up.

Bev placed a cup of coffee in front of her. "I thought you'd come in here dancing this morning. Pictured you doing one of those leap things and twirling all around. So what happened?"

They had been working together for the last year and Abby didn't hide anything about her relationship with Dean from her co-worker. They were friends and even though Bev was closer to Abby's mom's age, she still considered her to be one of her dearest friends.

So she told her all about what happened the previous evening – from the time Dean showed up to pick up Maya from class until they parted ways in the diner parking lot. It felt good to say it all out loud and when she was done, she let out a long breath.

"Am I wrong?" she asked quietly. "Is it wrong for me to want it all?"

Bev gave her a sympathetic smile. "No, sweetie, it's not wrong at all. You've worked hard and you've been very honest about your plans from the beginning. Maybe Dean was just feeling a little insecure and needed to know that you…you know, need him too."

"I do! I do need him," Abby argued. "But he made it all seem so…black-and-white! Like I was wrong to want both or…or…that I should just be happy that he's ready to settle down and it should be enough for me. We've never talked about what else I want for the future beyond this studio! Shouldn't he have at least talked to me about this?"

Rather than answer right away, Bev grabbed a couple of napkin dispensers and began filling them. After a few minutes, she looked at Abby. "Let me ask you something – does Dean Hayes strike you as a man who is a good communicator?"

"What?"

"I'm serious. Think about it. He's been on his own for a long time and before that, when he lived with his family, he pretty much kept to himself to stay under the radar." Reaching out, she put her hand over Abby's. "Most men suck at communicating, Abby. Like, they seriously suck at it. I've been married for over thirty years and I can say this with great certainty. I think Dean was just feeling a little left out and he just sort of…acted like a man."

"And what does that mean exactly?"

"A jerk. He acted like a jerk," Bev said flatly.

"No argument there," Abby murmured and then sighed. "So what am I supposed to do?"

"If it were me, I'd give yourself a couple of days to calm down and hopefully he's doing the same. You're going to see him when he picks up Maya from ballet classes so it's not like you're going to be avoiding each other, right?"

"Not that I know of."

"Trust me. Sometimes everyone just needs to retreat to their corners and think things through. By this time next week, you're going to be fine. I know it."

"I hope you're right."

"Abby, I've been in your shoes enough times to know that the old adage is true – absence makes the heart grow fonder." She smiled. "Give him a little time and Dean will realize that he was wrong."

While Bev walked away, Abby stayed in her seat and thought about what she'd just heard.

It made sense. Sort of. And really, the time apart was exactly what she'd recommended to Dean last night so maybe it was the right thing to do.

She just didn't want them to be apart for too long.

****

Patti Foster showed up in Silver Bell Falls the day before the big Christmas recital and was instantly concerned.

"Oh, Abby," she said when she first saw her daughter, "you're working too hard. Look at you! Are you eating or sleeping at all?"

They were standing in baggage claim waiting for her mother's luggage and it was the last place Abby wanted to be having this conversation.

Or any conversation for that matter.

She had taken the last couple of days off from the diner to get ready for the recital and luckily, her mother had taken the red-eye flight so that Abby could be back in Silver Bell in time for her afternoon rehearsals.

"Abigail," her mother stated firmly, "you are going to be of no use to your students if you are falling down because you aren't taking care of yourself."

"I'm fine, mom," Abby said distractedly, watching the carousel for the incoming luggage. "Is that your purple suitcase with the yellow ribbon on the handle?"

Patti was wise to her daughter's distraction tactics. "You know it is." But before she could go and get it for herself, Abby stepped over and grabbed the luggage. "I only have the one bag."

With a nod, Abby walked toward the exit. Mentally she worked out how long it would take to get back to town and have lunch at the diner before getting her mom settled in so she could head to the community center for rehearsals.

They walked in silence.

They even drove for the first thirty minutes in silence.

Patti was the first to speak.

"Have you tried calling him?" she asked finally.

It was pointless to pretend that she didn't know who her mother was talking about. "No."

"And why not?"

"I kind of took the hint when he didn't drive Maya to classes last week or pick her up. He had Kathy Jones do it and don't think people didn't notice. So then I had to deal with all of the inquiring minds who wanted to know what went wrong." She sighed. "I thought, okay, he just needs a little more time. And then this week he did come and pick her up, but he waited at the door and wouldn't come more than a foot into the classroom."

"So again I have to wonder why you haven't called him to talk about it. Maybe he's waiting for you to make the first move."

"And maybe I'm waiting for him to apologize for being such a jerk!" Abby snapped. Then she felt guilty – after all, it wasn't her mother's fault – and immediately apologized. "I went over and said hello to him and talked to him about the rehearsals and about the recital and he barely said two words to me. I swear, it reminded me of when I first started working at the diner and met him. It's infuriating!"

"Abby, sometimes you have to be the one to make the first move, even if you don't want to."

It took everything she had not to scream in frustration. Instead, Abby mentally counted to ten before responding. "I have spent a large portion of my life being the one to make the first move whether I was in the wrong or not. For once – just once – I'd like someone else to make the first move, especially someone who claims to be in love with me! Is that too much to ask?"

"Abby…"

"Mom, if I give in to this, it's just going to set a precedent for the future. Dean will do something that hurts me – hurts my feelings – and I'll be the one going to him to make it right. Well, you know what? It's not right. It's not okay."

"Is it right that you're cutting off your nose to spite your face?" her mother asked evenly.

Leave it to a mom to come back with logic. And Abby was old enough to know that she wasn't going to win this argument. Or discussion. Or whatever it was they were having. A change of subject was in order.

Again.

"I told Bev we'd stop in for lunch when we got back to town," she said pleasantly. "Dan even made your favorite – chicken-fried steak!"

"Well isn't he sweet?" Patti said with a big smile, not in the least bit fooled – again – by her daughter's change of subject. "What's the plan for the rest of the day?"

"After lunch we'll go to the house and get you settled and then you can drop me off at the community center and that's where I'll be until about nine tonight."

"And this is why you look like hell," her mother murmured.

"Excuse me?"

"When are you going to eat dinner?"

"I was planning on packing a sandwich," Abby said with a hint of defiance. "And an apple."

Patti chuckled softly. "Do you really need to be there that late? Are you holding rehearsals up until that time? It seems a little too late for younger ones to be out on a school night."

"The last group will take the stage by eight but I'll be there until nine straightening up and getting things ready for tomorrow."

"I thought you had volunteers for that."

Abby shrugged. "I feel better if I'm there with them."

"No one likes a control freak, Abby."

Ugh. Why had she thought it would be fun to have her mother in town for the recital? Another mental count and she was ready to respond. "I'm not being a control freak, Mom. I'm making sure that we have everything we need for tomorrow night. It's my recital, my classes, my students. I need to oversee everything."

"I'm not going to split hairs with you," Patti said with a long-suffering sigh. "I'll just plan to pick you up at ten."

"Nine. I said I'd be done at nine."

Patti shrugged. "I have a feeling it will be closer to ten. If you're done sooner, call me and I'll come and get you. I just hope I'll still be awake. I was up very early today. Didn't sleep very well on the plane either."

Oh Lord, she thought. Here we go…

"Fine! I'll leave at eight and let the volunteers do their thing. They all know that you're here so I'm sure it will be fine."

Reaching over, Patti gently pat her daughter's hand. "Thank you, sweetheart. I appreciate that." With a happy sigh, she relaxed in her seat. "So tell me about Maya. Did you already get her a Christmas present?"

# Thirteen

"Abby, go!" Kathy Jones said with a sympathetic smile. "Everyone's been picked up and we've just got a few things left to do here. I'm sure your mom is already outside waiting for you. Go and spend some time with her."

Doing her best not to roll her eyes or complain about how pleasant the last six hours had been without spending time with her mom, Abby simply said thank you and went to grab her gym bag. Truth be told, she was tired. Exhausted, really. She hadn't slept well in weeks and she was fairly certain that it was partially responsible for her short temper with her mother. Normally the two of them got along like best friends so it had to be the stress and lack of sleep.

With a final wave to the girls, Abby walked out to the lobby as she slipped her coat on. Maybe tonight would be the night that she finally slept. Maybe tonight would be the night she didn't lay in bed and stare at the ceiling until she thought she'd go mad.

And maybe tonight would be the night that she didn't curse being alone.

Sure. And maybe tonight would be the night she learned that Santa was real and saw reindeer fly.

"I think I'm getting delirious," she murmured, stepping out into the cold night air. There were some light snow flurries blowing around and she felt bad because her mom hated driving in the snow. "Figures."

Slipping her hands into her pockets, Abby looked around the parking lot but didn't see her mother anywhere. They had said eight o'clock and it was only eight-fifteen, so where was she?

Off in the distance, she saw a pair of headlights coming her way and sighed with relief. Her mother knew her too well and probably figured to come a little late since it wasn't feasible for her to be out the door at eight o'clock exactly.

With a slight shiver, Abby adjusted the strap of her gym bag on her shoulder, straightened her posture and put a smile on her face and…

Realized it wasn't her mother pulling into the parking lot.

Dammit.

The car turned just before the entrance to the lot.

With her smile gone, Abby pulled out her cell phone, quickly scrolled to her mother's number and hit send. Maybe she really was tired and had fallen asleep. The phone rang and rang and rang and even though Abby's first response was panic, she knew there was a very real, very logical explanation for her mother not to answer.

"Okay…now what?"

She could always go back inside and ask one of the girls to drive her home, but they were busy and now Abby was starting to feel a little anxious. Looking in the direction of the diner, she decided to run over and see who was working so maybe someone there could give her a ride. She made it as far as halfway across the parking lot when a car pulled in.

"Thank God," she said quietly, thinking for a minute that it was her mother. The lights were a little bit blinding and once it got closer, she groaned. Not her car. Not her mother. "Damn." It was cold and she was tired and all she wanted was to get home so she started walking again. The car pulled up beside her and she gasped when she turned.

It was Dean.

Great.

"Where's your car?" he asked with a hint of annoyance.

For a minute, she wanted to be snarky and say something about how his sweet words made her heart flutter but opted against it. "My mother has it. She was supposed to be here to pick me up but she's late and she's not answering the phone."

"So you're going to walk home? That seems a little crazy. It's twenty degrees out there."

"Really? I hadn't noticed," she snapped back and then started to walk again.

"Abby? Come on. Get in and I'll drive you home."

Again, she wanted to argue, but it was more important to get home and make sure her mother was all right. So she climbed into the car with a mumbled thanks. When Dean didn't move or start to drive, she looked over at him expectantly.

"Uh…Dean? This is the part where you actually drive me home." Yeah, she knew she was being bitchy but the last thing she needed today was to deal with him – especially when she was already emotionally on edge.

His expression was neutral – much like he used to look at her before they started dating – and it made her heart hurt a little. When he finally nodded and turned to face forward again, Abby tried to tell herself that she was relieved.

But she wasn't.

She wanted to talk to him – to reach out and touch him and feel his arms around her – but that wasn't possible. And she was just too damn tired to do anything about it right now anyway. Maybe after the recital they'd finally have a moment to talk. Then she remembered the parade was on Saturday. Okay, so maybe after that.

Yes. Yes, definitely after that.

Feeling like she had made the right decision, Abby quietly sighed and relaxed in her seat and closed her eyes for just a moment.

\*\*\*\*

Dean parked the car in the driveway and looked over at Abby and smiled.

She was asleep.

It was no wonder. She looked exhausted and he knew for a fact that she was working way too hard. From what everyone in Silver Bell told him, she was pushing herself too hard – just as she did every year at this time – and they were all worried about her.

So was he.

"Abby? Abby, you need to wake up. We're home," he said softly.

She hummed a little and turned toward him but didn't open her eyes. Dean smiled because this was what she normally did when he tried to wake her up. It always took a little coaxing to get her to open her eyes, but he didn't think it would be appropriate for him to try and wake her up the way he'd done in the past.

Gently, he shook her shoulder. "Abby?"

"Mmft…"

He chuckled softly. "Abby? I don't see your car here. We need to go inside and see what's going on."

That woke her up. She quickly sat up and looked around. Her eyes were wide and a little dazed. "What? The car's not…oh my God!" She climbed out of the car and ran up to the front door as she pulled her phone from her pocket.

Dean followed and took her keys from her hands when she kept missing the lock. "Let me."

"C'mon, Mom," she murmured into the phone. "Pick up. Just pick up the phone."

Opening the door, Dean ushered her inside and shut the door behind them.

"Why won't she answer the damn phone?" Abby cried out and looked at him in complete dismay. "Did you see my car on the side of the road on the way here?"

"Don't you think I would have stopped if I had?" he asked, calmly and evenly.

"I think I should call Josiah…call the police…call someone! Obviously something's happened and…" She turned around when Dean tapped her on the shoulder and held out his phone. "What? Did you already call Josiah?" She grabbed the phone. "Josiah? My mother is missing! I need you to…"

"Oh for crying out loud, Abigail, there's no need to call the sheriff."

"Mom?!" she cried and then looked at Dean in confusion. "Where are you? How did Dean know how to reach you? Why weren't you answering my calls?"

"One question at a time and…wait a minute…yes, Maya, you can have the last cookie. Go ahead, sweetheart." She paused and then said, "I forgot how little oncs can totally manipulate you into giving them just about anything, but she's so darn cute that I don't even mind giving her whatever she wants."

"You're with Maya?" Abby asked in confusion, still looking at Dean.

His expression was mildly amused but he could tell that Abby wasn't feeling quite the same way.

"Why…how did you end up with Maya?"

"I ran into Dean after I dropped you off at the community center earlier."

"Oh really? Where?"

"At his house," her mother replied levelly. "It's such a lovely home and their tree is magnificent!"

"Mom, focus! Why would you do that?"

"Compliment the tree? Because it's beautiful. You know I've always loved a live tree. I don't do one back in Arizona but…"

Abby sighed loudly. "Mom…"

"Sweetheart, I need to go. Maya and I are going to read a story while we finish our milk. Go and talk to Dean and I'll talk to you later."

Before Abby could say anything, Patti hung up.

Without waiting for her to say anything, Dean took the phone from her hands and put it in his pocket. "So she's all right," he said lightly.

Abby's gaze narrowed at him and rather than responding, she spun and walked away, shedding her coat and tossing it on the chair that sat in the corner of her living room. He knew he needed to give her a minute and when she began to pace he feared that maybe this whole idea wasn't so great.

"She didn't mean to worry you," he began. "I guess we didn't think that you'd get upset about it."

The pacing immediately stopped. "Didn't think I'd…?" With a growl of frustration, she came right at him. "She was late, wouldn't answer her phone and the car was gone! What conclusion should I have come to?"

"Okay, okay…you're absolutely right," he said calmly. "At the time we didn't really think about that."

"Of course not. Because that would mean you were actually thinking about me and my feelings," Abby snapped.

Yeah. He deserved that one.

"Do you have any idea…"

"I'm sorry," Dean interrupted. It wasn't quick, it wasn't hurried, it wasn't even a plea. Hell, it was barely a whisper.

Abby looked at him and the fight seemed to go out of her instantly. Wordlessly, she walked over to the couch and sat down. Dean hated confrontation, which was probably why he ended up living the way he did for most of his life. Maybe if he'd spoken up and told his sister and his parents – and everyone – how he hated being compared to his wild sibling, he'd be a different person right now.

Looking at Abby, he sighed and prayed that maybe she still loved the person he was right now.

"You were right," he said quietly. "I had gone and worked everything out in my head and just thought you'd feel the same way."

"I did...I do feel the same way," she instantly corrected. "But asking me to give up my dream isn't fair, Dean."

He nodded. "I don't want you to give it up, Abby. I swear I don't." Looking at her pleadingly, he reached out and took one of her hands in his. "I just need to know that I'm part of that dream."

A small chuckle was her first response. "Of course you're part of that dream! You're the best part of it all. When I look at everything – the big picture – you're there with me. You and Maya. I couldn't do this alone. I don't want to do this alone."

"But you're not. You have just about every person in Silver Bell Falls right there with you. I think you single-handedly made this close-knit town even closer."

She laughed again. "And really, I had nothing to do with it. That was all Millie's work."

Shaking his head, he lifted her hand to his lips and kissed it. "No. It's you, Abby. You have given so much to so many people and this is their way of giving a little something back to you. They all love you."

"There's only one person's love that I want," she said quietly as she inched just a little bit closer to him.

"You have it," he replied just before he captured her lips with his.

It was like coming home.

With his arms slowly banding around her, Dean pulled her into his lap and simply kept kissing her. It went from a sweet I-missed-you kind of kiss to a hard, demanding one that had him losing himself in the taste of her, the heat of her.

Hell, everything about her.

It would be the easiest thing in the world to lay her down right here on the couch, strip her and make love to her and just forget about everything else for a little while.

But he couldn't.

Not until they worked things out and knew where each other stood.

Just the thought of losing her terrified the shit out of him.

Reluctantly, he ended the kiss and reveled in the feeling of Abby melting against him as she caught her breath.

"I missed you," she whispered against his neck.

He hugged her close. "I missed you too."

Abby pulled back and looked him in the face. "Where do we go from here?"

Dean heard the uncertainty in her voice and it just about gutted him. For almost two weeks he'd had nothing to do but think about their situation. He'd lost count of the number of people who came and gave him advice, but the best advice came from Josiah.

Typical.

"You have to decide what you can and can't live with," Josiah told him. "It's really as simple as that."

"It can't be that simple," Dean had argued.

"When Melanie moved here, she hated everything about the town – the cold, the location – and Christmas. I never saw myself living any place else but here. Never wanted to leave. But if it came down to leaving here so I could be with her? I would have left."

"Okay, I see where you're going with that, but…it's not really the same thing."

"Yes, it is," Josiah countered. "Abby has always wanted to have her own dance studio. Everyone in town knew that. You knew that. Are you saying you won't be with her – would give up having a life with her – because she now owns a dance studio? Wasn't her dancing one of the things that attracted you to her in the first place?"

It was.

"Dean?"

Abby's voice pulled him back to the present.

"I still want all of the things I wanted before," he said honestly. "I want to marry you. Have a family with you." Taking her hand in his, he kissed it again. "I love you, Abby."

A slow smile crossed her face. "And what about the dance studio?"

"I want to be a part of that. I want to help you with it and work on it with you and be there at the end of the day to celebrate all of its successes with you."

"You know it's going to require a lot of hours right now. Well, not right now, but after the New Year it's going to be a little bit crazy, even with all of the help."

"And I want to be there to hear all about the craziness. Actually, I want to be standing beside you in the midst of the craziness." With his free hand, he reached up and caressed her cheek. "Am I too late? Did I mess this all up?"

Her smile grew and as she leaned forward and rested her forehead against his, she almost purred. "You're not too late. And you know what? I think we both messed up. So I'm sorry too."

"You have nothing to apologize for," he replied gruffly.

"I love you, Dean." A nervous laugh bubbled out of her and she straightened again. "I still can't believe that I get to say that."

He couldn't help but smile at her admission. "Why? What's wrong with that?"

"For so long, I never thought that you'd ever even notice me. And then after we started dating I still figured it would be a long time before you were ready for anything more. I had myself convinced that I would just have to tell you I loved you in my head. But I like saying it out loud to you so much more."

"Not as much as I like hearing it."

For a minute they were both content to sit and hold each other, but Abby broke the silence first. "So um…my mom is over with Maya, huh?"

He nodded.

"When do you need to get back?"

"Do you want my opinion or what your mom told me?"

Abby laughed, her head falling back. "Oh…I'm almost afraid to ask."

"I told her I wouldn't be late," he began. "And her response was that she'd already spent one night sleeping on an airplane and she would be just fine spending another night sleeping on a couch." He chuckled. "Then she tested the couch and confirmed that she could sleep there with no worries."

Hiding her face on his shoulder now, Dean could feel Abby's body vibrating with laughter. "Only my mom…"

"So the way I see it…"

He never got to finish. Abby hopped off of his lap, took him by the hand and led him to her bedroom. "We have plenty of time," she said once they were next to the bed.

"That's a good thing because I have plenty that I want to do," he growled before kissing her again.

****

"This is good."

"Mm-hmm…"

"You don't have to leave yet, do you?"

Dean lifted his head and looked at the clock. "It's almost five. I want to be home before Maya wakes up."

Placing a light kiss on Dean's chest, Abby sighed. "You're a good dad."

"I don't know about that, but I'm learning."

"Trust me. You're a good dad and Maya's lucky to have you." Another kiss. "And I'm lucky to have you too."

Hugging her close, he placed a light kiss on the top of her head. "Did you sleep at all last night?"

Abby laughed softly. "Yes. I think after that second time, I slipped into a coma and I was there until about ten minutes ago. It was wonderful."

"Today's going to be crazy for you, huh?"

She nodded. "And tomorrow. The parade is always a little bit like controlled chaos. There isn't a lot that the girls need to do other than ride on the float and wave to the crowd but there's normally some anxiety about it and I need to be there to keep everyone calm and smiling."

"Maya's so excited about that. I think she's looking forward to that more than the recital."

She laughed again. "She's enthusiastic about them both. Today she'll be all about the recital but as soon as the curtain closes, she'll be all about the parade."

"Do you have plans for after the parade?"

"As a matter of fact I do."

"Oh." There was no mistaking the disappointment in his voice.

Leaning up, Abby looked down at his face and took pity on him. "My plan was to walk around and look at all the crafts and have some lunch with you and Maya and my mom and then come back here for dinner. That is...if you're interested."

He pulled her down on top of him and then rolled them over until she was on her back beneath him. "Sweetheart, wherever you are, that's where I'll be. Forever."

"I like the sound of that."

Looking over his shoulder at the clock one more time, Dean considered his options. Then, with a wicked smile, he looked down at Abby. "I have an hour before I have to leave. I know I should let you sleep but..."

Her hand snaked up around his neck and gently pulled his head down to hers. "I can't think of a better way to start my day."

"Get used to it," he murmured, right before he kissed her.

****

It was frigid outside. If Abby had to guess, she'd say it was the coldest day of the year so far – and that was saying something.

The parade was finally ending and she never thought she'd be so happy to see the end of the route. Things had gotten changed around and other than Santa being the final float of the day, somehow her little group of dancers ended up on the float right in front of him. Normally they were near the front of the parade but because of the change in order, it meant everyone was outside longer and everyone was getting antsy.

Including her.

Okay, especially her.

The idea of climbing off the float and getting warm was enough to make her giddy.

The girls were all smiling and waving to the crowd and everyone was cheering for them. They had done an amazing job in their recital the previous night. The entire show had been a complete success and she was so full of pride that she thought her heart would simply burst.

Her littlest girls were at the front of the float and they were huddled together and giggling. When Maya turned and waved at her, Abby had to fight the urge to just walk over and embrace her.

Maya did it. She was a real ballerina last night and after her group performed and they came backstage, Maya had jumped into Abby's arms smiling from ear to ear.

"I did it! I did it! I did it!" she'd cried. "And I only messed up once!"

"You did a great job, Maya Papaya! I'm so proud of you!"

All around her were her youngest girls, all dressed in red dresses and red satin ballet slippers. They looked so festive and happy and really, she was thrilled with how well they had performed.

Dean had come backstage – even though parents were encouraged to wait until all of the performances were done – and handed Maya a bouquet of flowers. It was incredibly sweet and when he picked her up and hugged her, Abby could only stand back in awe.

They'd come a long way. In two short months they had begun to fully adapt to this new life. They had been whispering to each other while Abby had gotten the next group of dancers ready. When the curtain rose, she'd stepped back until she was close to the two of them and heard the most heart-wrenching question.

"Do you think my mom and dad saw me, Uncle Dean? Do you think they were clapping when I finished?"

While she was certain Dean answered and told her yes, Abby had to step away and fight back tears. That was not a question a five-year-old should have to ask. Even though she asked it very conversationally, Abby knew it was something that weighed on her heart.

Thank God for Dean. Thank God for all the people here in Silver Bell Falls who had embraced her. And she was thankful that Christmas was only a week away and she was going to be surrounded by people who loved Maya and wanted to make this her best Christmas ever.

Including Abby and her mom.

It was going to be a great Christmas.

The parade float was slowing down and Abby breathed a sigh of relief. The mayor began making a speech thanking all of the volunteers who helped with the parade and the craft fair. Then he went on to give instructions for where everyone could grab some lunch in a heated tent. Every year he made the announcement and every year Abby thought it was unnecessary. The people of Silver Bell Falls knew how to maneuver around town on parade day.

The girls were getting restless as the float came to a stop and she reminded everyone to stay where they were until their helpers came over to assist.

"It will be just a few more minutes," she said quietly. "And once we have people here to help us down…"

She stopped speaking when the voice over the PA system changed. When did the mayor hand off the mic?

Listening for a moment, she froze.

She knew that voice.

She loved that voice.

"Abigail Foster, you are everything to me."

Oh. My. God. What was he doing?

When she finally spotted him, he was walking through the crowd toward the float. When he stepped up on it and scooped Maya up into his arms, she saw that he had a red Santa hat on his head and she couldn't help but laugh at how utterly adorable he looked.

They stepped up to her, both smiling like they had a secret. Dean looked at Maya and she nodded. Then they looked at her. Maya took the microphone from his hands.

"Abby, remember the first time we had dinner at your house and we said grace?" She didn't wait for Abby to respond, she just kept on going. "I told God that I was thankful to have a family to eat dinner with. Uncle Dean says that we're going to be a real family and I can't wait for you to move in with us and be with us all the time. Then we can dance together every day!"

She handed the microphone back to Dean.

"And I can't wait to see you dance every day," he said with just enough of a husky tone that made Abby blush. "I know that we talked about it but…I think it's important to do this the right way."

The gasp was out before she could stop it as Dean got down on one knee with Maya at his side. She held the microphone for him as he pulled a small velvet box from his pocket and held it out to her, opening it.

"We love you, Abby!" Maya said excitedly and her voice sounded so loud that it took a minute for Abby to realize that the entire town was watching and listening. She took a quick look around and saw what looked like hundreds of smiling faces.

Looking back at Dean – her vision slightly blurred by unshed tears – she smiled.

He was grinning too. "Yes, we do love you," he said as Maya held the microphone close to his mouth. "And we would be honored if you'd marry me – marry us – and make us a real family."

"I will," she said and in the blink of an eye, she was in Dean's arms and being kissed thoroughly as the town cheered all around them.

# Epilogue

*Christmas Day…*

"You really outdid yourself, Mom," Abby said as she sat back in her chair. "I swear every year this just totally makes my day."

Patti smiled as she stood and began to clear the table. "It's our tradition and we've had a lot of practice with it. I would think you'd want something else by now."

"Are you kidding? Cinnamon pumpkin waffles…we only have them once a year. Why would I change that?"

"I guess you're right. It does make them a little extra special when you only have them once a year." Patti smiled at Maya who was finishing hers. "What did you think of them, Maya? Do you think you could enjoy having this as a special Christmas breakfast?"

They were all sitting at Dean's kitchen table in their pajamas after starting their day at sunrise. Abby leaned against Dean and watched as Maya gave a thumbs up as she finished her last bite of waffle.

"I think that's a seal of approval," Abby said, then looked over her shoulder at Dean. "What about you? Did you like them?"

"I ate four of them," he said with a laugh. "I think it's safe to say that we found our next Christmas tradition."

"Whew!" Patti said and then looked at her daughter. "Now you can definitely marry him."

She was marrying Dean.

In five days.

Abby still couldn't believe it. After his very public proposal, they had been approached by just about everyone – first to offer congratulations and next to offer suggestions for a very festive New Year's Day wedding. While it hadn't been something Abby thought she'd ever consider – especially after the argument she and Dean had had weeks ago – now that things had calmed down, she realized that she didn't want to wait.

Even now, she was essentially living with him. Both Abby and her mother had spent the night at Dean's so they could be there to see Maya first thing in the morning when she came out to see what Santa brought her.

A ballerina doll.

A new coat.

New ballet slippers.

And then about a dozen other gifts including clothes, a dollhouse, a new sled and...

"Snuffles, no!" Maya said firmly. "You can't lick the plate! Syrup isn't good for dogs!" Then she looked at Dean and Abby. "Wait, is it?"

"Definitely not," Dean said and shook his head. Turning his head, he whispered in Abby's ear, "What were we thinking? A puppy? Now?"

A soft laugh was her only response.

Snuffles was a very energetic pug puppy and was now officially a member of the family.

"Maybe we should take him for a walk, Maya?" Patti suggested. "And then when we come back you can give him a treat."

"Yeah!" She immediately jumped up and ran to her room to get dressed.

"Mom, it's freezing out. You don't have to go. I'll go out with her," Abby said, but as soon as she started to rise, Patti stopped her.

"Nonsense. I'm going to be staying here and taking care of Maya and Snuffles while you're on your honeymoon so I might as well get in the habit now."

"Mom…"

"Oh hush. Let me go and get dressed. But I will let you finish cleaning up," she said with a grin as she walked out of the kitchen. Five minutes later, Patti, Maya and Snuffles were out the door.

Abby stood at the sink and was rinsing the dishes when Dean came up behind her, wrapping his arms around her waist and nuzzling her neck. "A week from now we'll get to do this without worrying about anyone walking in on us."

"Washing dishes?" she teased. "I was hoping to get away from that for a few days."

Throwing his head back and laughing, Dean hugged her tighter. "Smart ass. You know what I mean."

She turned in his arms and looped her arms around his neck. "I certainly do and believe me, I am looking forward to it. I already have something special to wear to dance for you in."

His expression instantly sobered. "Really?"

She nodded.

"Is it white and lacy?"

"I'm not telling."

"Black and lacy?"

Chuckling, she rested her head against his chest. "Still not telling."

"Ooh…I bet it's red and lacy."

"I'm beginning to notice a trend here…"

"Okay, fine. No more questions. Just tell me this…is it something I'll have to apologize for if I rip it?"

That was still one of her favorite sexy memories. "Not at all. Actually, I think I'm encouraging that."

"Duly noted."

Holding each other close, Abby felt like the luckiest woman alive. She had so much to be thankful for this year and they had so much to look forward to that she finally understood what Dean said to her not that long ago.

Now that she knew what she wanted – what was waiting for her – for the rest of her life, she was anxious to get it started as soon as possible.

"Is it weird that I think it's too quiet in here?" he asked.

"Not at all. I feel that way too."

"C'mon. Let's go and get dressed so that when they get back we can go out and try out our new sleds."

"I can't wait! I haven't gone sleigh riding in years!"

"Me either – which is kind of why I got the sleds. I know it was a little selfish of me, but…"

"Nonsense. We're all going to enjoy them. Trust me."

Thirty minutes later, they were all laughing hysterically as they slid down the hill at the back of Dean's property. Abby watched as Dean pulled Maya and her sled back up to the top as the little girl begged him to hurry up so she could go again.

Clearly, they all had a little bit of a problem with patience.

And as they lined up on their sleds at the top of the hill, Abby looked from Dean to Maya and back again and grinned.  They may not be big on patience but they were definitely big on love.

"Come on you guys!" Maya called.  "I'll race you to the bottom!"

"You're on!" Dean challenged, but Abby let them each start just a wee bit ahead of her.  It was much more fun to hang back and watch them and listen to them laugh.  When they reached the bottom, they turned and cheered her on as she sped toward them.

Which was exactly how she felt about her life right now.

She was speeding toward the future and the two of them were standing there waiting for her with open arms.

####

# Also by Samantha Chase

**The Enchanted Bridal Series:**

The Wedding Season

Friday Night Brides

The Bridal Squad

Glam Squad & Groomsmen

**The Montgomery Brothers Series:**

Wait for Me

Trust in Me

Stay with Me

More of Me

Return to You

Meant for You

I'll Be There

Until There Was Us

Suddenly Mine

## The Shaughnessy Brothers Series:

Made for Us

Love Walks In

Always My Girl

This is Our Song

Sky Full of Stars

Holiday Spice


## Band on the Run Series:

One More Kiss

One More Promise

One More Moment


## The Christmas Cottage Series:

The Christmas Cottage

Ever After

## Silver Bell Falls Series:

Christmas in Silver Bell Falls

Christmas On Pointe

A Very Married Christmas

## Life, Love & Babies Series:

The Baby Arrangement

Baby, Be Mine

Baby, I'm Yours

## Preston's Mill Series:

Roommating

Speed Dating

Complicating

## 7 Brides for 7 Soldiers

Ford

## The Protectors Series:

Protecting His Best Friend's Sister

Protecting the Enemy

Protecting the Girl Next Door

Protecting the Movie Star


## Standalone Novels

Jordan's Return

Catering to the CEO

In the Eye of the Storm

A Touch of Heaven

Moonlight in Winter Park

Wildest Dreams

Going My Way

Going to Be Yours

Waiting for Midnight

Seeking Forever

Mistletoe Between Friends

Snowflake Inn

Samantha Chase is a New York Times and USA Today bestseller of contemporary romance. She released her debut novel in 2011 and currently has more than forty titles under her belt! When she's not working on a new story, she spends her time reading romances, playing way too many games of Scrabble or Solitaire on Facebook, wearing a tiara while playing with her sassy pug Maylene…oh, and spending time with her husband of 25 years and their two sons in North Carolina.

## Where to Find Me:

**Website:** www.chasing-romance.com

**Facebook:** www.facebook.com/SamanthaChaseFanClub

**Twitter:** https://twitter.com/SamanthaChase3

Sign up for my mailing list and get exclusive content and chances to win members-only prizes!

http://bit.ly/1jqdxPR

CPSIA information can be obtained
at www.ICGtesting.com
Printed in the USA
LVHW041411281119
638727LV00019B/1935/P